Seventh Son

A.M. Offenwanger

AMOVITAM PRESS

amovitam press

2nd Edition

Note: This book uses Canadian spelling and punctuation.

Also by A.M. Offenwanger

THE SEPTIMUS SERIES
Seventh Son
Cat and Mouse
Lavender's Blue (A Septimus Short Story)
Checkmate
Star Bright

Standalone:
Martin Millerson: A Retelling of "Puss in Boots"

Novellas:
The Twelve Days of Christmas: A Tale of Christmastide.
With Elves.
The Forty-Dollar Christmas: A Canadian Holiday Story

FOREWORD TO THE SECOND EDITION

I wrote *Seventh Son* in 2011, and published it in 2014. It was the first novel I ever wrote and published. I was quite proud of it at that time, and went on to write and publish several more books in the series. But after ten years of writing, and of editing for other writers, I re-read this book, and I realized that while I still really enjoyed the story, I could do a lot better on the writing front, and that this book deserved a makeover.

So, if you read *Seventh Son* before, rest assured that this is still the same story and that nothing has changed about Cat and Guy and all the people you've met before (except that perhaps they're a bit less diffident and wordy). I hope you enjoy this new version just as much.

And if this is the first time you're here, then Welcome! I hope you'll find a home in the Septimus World.

Angelika M. Offenwanger
September 2025

This is for Steve.
And for Anna, because she started it all,
and then suggested I dedicate it to Steve.

Contents

CHAPTER 1

I T WAS THE BLUE bowl that started it all. Not the blue-and-white Ming one right next to it, nor the dull green pottery frog that sat at the front of the display cabinet, goggling up at Catriona out of its little brown pottery eyes. No, the blue pottery bowl.

It was a turquoise blue, very much like the eyes of the weird guy who had stared at Cat in the Room of Local Antiquities so hard she left the room as quickly as she could without looking like she was running, which brought her to the Ceramics Room and the case with the blue bowl. She was almost sure the guy had already followed her into Local Antiquities; she had seen him out of the corner of her eye when she was admiring the big sculpture of the two lovers in the Marble Room.

Cat had first noticed the man outside near the bus loop because of his unusual outfit: an odd khaki vest over top of a shirt of unbleached cotton, if not linen, and pants that looked like they were made of well-worn leather—not the kind that leather jackets are made of, but more like the thin, buff-coloured leather you used for polishing cars. But

1

what had been most noticeable about him were his eyes. They were the most startling colour, not blue, not green, but a brilliant turquoise. Just like the semi-precious stone. And that bowl.

Cat had been looking at a hand-woven basket made of two different colours of reed, crafted by a local artisan circa 1857 (or so the label claimed), when she felt those disconcerting turquoise eyes on her. The man stood next to a display of mummified food (to be consumed by the dearly departed in the afterlife, one assumed), clear across the other side of the room by the opposite entrance at the rounded archway, and just stared.

The stare made Cat really uneasy. What did he want from her? Was her bra strap showing? Or did she look weirder than she thought in her green-and-blue-tiered gypsy skirt and hand-embroidered peasant blouse? She had thought she could get away with that outfit; after all, she was on holiday.

She pretended to look back at the woven basket, then nonchalantly moved over to the next display cabinet—another basket, this one from 1863 (how did they even know that? Had someone sat beside the weaver with a notebook and taken down the exact stardate of the creation?)—and sidled through the archway into the next room.

The display case with the blue bowl was a third of the way across the room, around the corner from the doorway. Cat moved over to it to get out of the line of sight from Local Antiquities, glancing out of the corner of her eye to see if the man was following her—not yet, thank goodness—and then gave her attention to the display cabinet.

It was an unusual case, open-topped, not completely encased in glass like the other displays, and lined with a dark brown velvety material. The frog sat at the front (it was nearly three thousand years old, its label stated); behind it, held up by the two claws of a wire plate stand, was a shallow blue-and-white bowl with a rounded lip (Chinese, Thirteenth Century AD, From the Collection of Mr. and Mrs. Arthur Schlipfengrimmler, Generous Patrons of the Sammelhauser Museum).

And off to the side, almost as if it didn't belong, the bowl. No label, no special display stand. Just the bowl on the brown velvet surface. It was not very big, no more than eight inches across and about half as high; the sides curved up steeply, and the lip turned inward, as if it were cupping a secret in its depths.

Cat leaned over the cabinet.

A little warning bell sounded in the back of her mind, a brief vision flitting through her head of the infrared sensors setting off the alarm, security guards bursting through the doors amidst a wail of sirens, to arrest her and drag her off to the police precinct to be interrogated for hours on end by the art squad... (They had one of those, didn't they?) Perhaps the open-topped cabinet was a trap for unsuspecting thieves...

But the next moment that thought faded from her mind. The bowl pulled at her, drew her in. The glaze was such a peculiar, deep turquoise, it seemed to shimmer with iridescence; deep beneath its surface was a luminescence that gave the illusion of motion, like the cool, blue-green depths of a mountain lake Cat had seen on a long-ago summer holiday.

She leaned closer, her nose inches from the top of the bowl; her hair swung forward and brushed its top edge. (If the alarm was going to sound, surely it would have done so by now?)

The movement at the bottom of the bowl became more pronounced. Tiny, sparkly pinpricks of light flitted through the glaze, shooting across Cat's field of vision. The glaze at the bottom of the bowl began to swirl. (Swirl? How could a glaze swirl? This was a bowl, just a piece of pottery!) The minute light sparks gathered at the edges of Cat's vision, became a clockwise dance, whirling faster and faster in counter motion to the swirling pinpricks at the bottom of the bowl. Cat tried to pull back, to straighten up, to get her eyes away from the whirling and dancing and swirling and sparkling blue—yet she barely knew where "back" was anymore, and her convulsive movement pitched her straight forwards, then jerked her sideways. She flung out her arm to protect herself from the sharp corner of the cabinet (the three-thousand-year-old frog! Smashing it would mean years of jail, for sure!), but her hand met no glass, no edge, no hard surface at all...

...she kept falling, landed on her rear, and her fingers sank inches deep into the soft, crumbly soil of a forest floor.

The whirling stopped, and slowly Cat's surroundings came back into focus. She stared around her, trying to make sense of what she was seeing.

Brown columns, illuminated by slanting dappled light, resolved into tree trunks, straight and smooth, gnarly and twisted. Evergreens towered over her, interspersed with leafy trees which the back of Cat's mind immediately classified as oaks and something else it did not recognize. A cluster of low shrubs surrounded the tree trunks, viciously spiky viridian leaves crowding around bunches of crimson fruits of some kind. Cat became aware of the sound of bird song overhead and a soft chirping from the undergrowth, and the spicy scent of a forest floor that had been baking in the sun all afternoon filled her nostrils.

A forest floor? What was she doing in a forest?

One minute she was in the Sammelhauser, looking at an odd turquoise-coloured bowl in order to avoid an odd turquoise-eyed man, and now...

Cat shook her head, hard. Hallucinations—she was hallucinating, wasn't she? She squeezed her eyes shut, then blinked them open again.

It didn't work. The forest stayed firmly in place around her, birds singing, whatever-it-was chirping in the grasses, spiky shrubs menacing her with blood-red berries, her fingers buried in the soil where she had tried to break her fall...

Yuck! Cat jerked her hand free. Cool, moist, dark bits of dirt (and who knew what else!) clung to her fingers. She gave a little scream and convulsively shook her hand, to no avail—the soil stuck. Panicked, she slapped at it with her other hand, then jumped to her feet, beat at her skirt, and stamped her feet.

"Aaah—ah ah ah—help, someone help!" she yelped, her breath coming in gasps. "Help!"

No help came.

But then it intruded on her consciousness that the dirt had actually shaken loose from her hand, her stamping feet were on solid ground, and there was no more of that whirling, spinning, and swirling around her.

Cat slowed her frantic dance, then stopped entirely. She took a deep breath, then another for good measure, and clasped her trembling hands in front of her mouth.

"Okay, Cat, okay. Okay okay okay. What's going on? Where am I? What is happening to me?"

Was she imagining all this? No, the ground was too solid for that, the spice of the forest scent too real.

Had there been some drugs in that display case that she had inhaled by accident? Drugs could give you remarkably realistic hallucinations, couldn't they? But not by just getting an accidental whiff of them.

Or... A little shiver ran down her spine. That turquoise-eyed man with his piercing stare! Had he somehow hypnotized her, or put the evil eye on her? Cat shook her head. What nonsense. She didn't believe in hypnotism, much less the evil eye. Or anything else supernatural and fantastic like that.

Yet, here she was, in a magical forest...

Wait. What made her think it was magical? It could be quite an ordinary forest. These were normal-looking trees, with trunks and branches and leaves; those were common-sounding birds; and even the shrubs seemed harmless (true, those spiky leaves were scary-looking, but they weren't *doing* anything. At the moment). Nothing magi-cal—right?

Yet here she was.

Here she was, in a forest, and not the museum she had so innocently entered not half an hour ago. Whatever this forest was, it was not ordinary, normal, common, or un-fantastical. Something very weird had just happened.

"Ah—ah—ah..."

Stop it, Cat. She bit down on the knuckle of her index finger to force herself to calm down. That normally did the trick—had done so ever since she was six years old and had freaked herself out with reading stories of Baba Yaga and her scary house on chicken feet (it hadn't made her put down the book, but it helped her finish it).

Okay, think, Cat, think. What could have just happened? What *did* just happen? She'd bent over a cabinet, looked at a turquoise bowl, the bowl started swirling...

Yes, the bowl started swirling. Which was very, very weird, and didn't explain anything at all. And now here she was, in a forest.

It certainly seemed like it was a real forest. She took her knuckle out from between her teeth, raised her head, and looked around. To the left, more trees, more shrubs (purple berries with a dusty bloom on those, and the leaves were not frighteningly spiky). A look to the right showed several gnarly trunks, the leaves bright green, the branches interlaced as if they were shaking hands with each other, forming a loose screen.

Between them, another tree was visible, its trunk smooth rather than twisted and rough like its neighbours, the bark a curious colour, an almost blueish sheen. Some of its branches hung over that natural screen, creating a canopy over Cat's head.

She turned around. Behind her, the trees were thinning a little, forming a kind of archway leading out of the space she was in.

Her gaze travelled back to the screen and the strange blue tree. Blue? Trees weren't supposed to be blue! Even a blue spruce wasn't really blue, certainly not its bark. Not like this one.

Maybe that tree wasn't actually there, after all? That would prove it, wouldn't it? It would prove *something*, anyway.

Cat put out her hand, reaching through a hole in the interlaced tree branches. Those really were there; the leaves brushed her arm. But that blue one...

Her fingertips grazed the trunk, and a tingle shot up her arm.

Cat jumped back. Was that an electric charge? It hadn't been painful, just startling. Would it do that every time she touched it?

She stretched out her fingers again. Carefully... carefully... yet a little farther... make contact... and nothing happened. The tree felt like every other tree she had ever touched in her life (not that there had been that many).

Cat slowly ran her fingers down the bark, alert, prepared for the shock of another tingle, but none came. The tree felt solid, tree-like—and sticky.

Bother! She had stuck her thumb right into some pitch!

She made a face. Stuck in a magical forest, with magical pitch stuck to her.

This was *not* what she wanted when she gave up her comfortable position as Associate Librarian of the Greenward Falls Community Library (Programs for Children Every Tuesday and Thursday, No Registration Required; Free Internet Access With Library Membership or Guest Pass). So she got bored, even felt a bit stifled, wanted adventure—but this was coming it rather too strong!

Pitch. How did one get rid of pitch?

She narrowly avoided wiping her hand on her skirt—she knew that would ruin it, and she very much liked that skirt. Buying it had been the first step in her rebellious flight to freedom. In the back of her mind she could still hear Ryan's voice when they'd looked at the skirt in the pop-up shop in the mall, with the sneer he affected at anything that wasn't high fashion, wasn't some kind of fancy name brand, and especially was something that Cat liked: "God, who'd wear that kind of hippie junk?"

As soon as Cat had come home from that disastrous last date, after Ryan had informed her that she wasn't his kind of woman after all, after he told her as a parting gift that her style wasn't very feminine (by which, Cat assumed, he meant tight tops with plunging necklines and mini-skirts that didn't leave much to the imagination) and that he owed it to himself to be with a woman who appreciated his masculinity (she knew for a fact that gym-enhanced chest muscles, copious beers, and being foul-mouthed were part of that package), after he had sped away in his showy Maserati and Cat had slammed the door (then opened it again, just to slam it a second time more energetically) and finished giving her pillow a good soaking of tears, she had marched back out her door (closing it firmly but quietly this time), got on the next bus, ridden right back to the mall, and bought the skirt without even trying it on.

As it happened, it fit perfectly. She loved the way it swirled around her calves, loved how the blues and greens were set off by the brilliant strips of red separating each tier, which winked up at her every time she looked down.

So it was important that she hadn't got the pitch on the skirt, and she needed to get it off her fingers as soon as possible. Cat ran through her mental file of emergency cleaning procedures. Alcohol—alcohol would dissolve pitch, she remembered reading it in a reference book. Eau de cologne had an alcohol base, there was some in her purse.

The purse! Where was her purse?

Cat whirled in a circle. A dark green leather slouch bag, maybe she had missed seeing it among the leaves...

But no. No purse. No bag. No eau de cologne to wipe off pitch with; no comb, no paper tissues, lemon drops, e-book reader, notebook, erasable gel pen, tiny Swiss Army knife with nail file and tweezers and scissors; no money and cell phone and ID and key to her best friend's apartment. Not that she would need the key, unless this forest was directly behind the Tuscany Towers Residential Block where her luggage temporarily resided in Unit 122 (Bauer, Monica; No Advertising Flyers Please). Which it wasn't, as the only thing behind the Tuscany Towers was a parking lot (the cars pulling in and out had kept Cat awake most of last night). She must have dropped her purse when that whole bizarre swirly-whirly thing happened. Bother bother *botheration*!

So she was in a strange forest without her purse, with magical pitch on her fingers, and not the faintest idea where she was, how she got there, or how she could get back to where she came from. By comparison, being up a creek without a paddle sounded downright convenient.

Cat plopped herself back down on the forest floor in exasperation. And promptly got some dry leaves stuck to the pitch on her thumb.

"Ugh!!"

For the first time in her life Cat wished that all those novels who talked about the hero "swearing fluently for five minutes" had gone into more detail; she could really use a few good swearwords right now. It was either swear or cry, and she knew that if she started to cry, she wouldn't be able to stop.

"W h y — D i d — T h i s — H a v e — T o — H a p - pen—To—Me?" she muttered through clenched teeth, savagely picking at the leaves on her fingers with each word. "It's—Just—Not—Fair!"

But wait! The leaves were taking some of the pitch with them. This might work. She stuck her thumb back into the leaves, picked up more dried foliage, and rubbed it off again. After three or four rounds of this, the better part of the pitch had come off and only a sticky smear was left on the side of her thumb, no more than as if she had accidentally run a glue stick over it (which had happened before, making display posters for the library. It had seemed exciting at the time).

11

Very well. Time to take stock. She had no idea where she was. Still on Earth? Hardly. She had never seen bushes like the spiky red-berried ones anywhere, and that included the pictures in the numerous reference tomes and websites she had perused in the course of her six years at the library. The forest looked vaguely European, with those trees, the oaks and not-oaks that she still couldn't identify. Cat had fond memories of the forests in Europe; she had spent three magical weeks there in her high school senior year. No, not magical. Beautiful, wonderful, inspiring, never-to-be-forgotten, but not magical. Not like this was magical. Oh dear...

One more time. *Get a grip, Cat.* She was in a magical, non-earthly, vaguely European forest, with no sign of civilization anywhere.

Come to think of it, if there were a civilization, would she be able to get help there? Or would the inhabitants be hostile? Or—or perhaps they were giant insects... or worse yet, the place might be governed by regular insects, and she had inadvertently stepped on several of their ruler's aunties and cousins in her frantic dance to get the dirt off herself...

Cat pulled her imagination sternly back down to earth. Or the ground, at any rate. No need for crazy flights of fancy, no call to borrow trouble until trouble came to her. At least that's what her grandma had always told her when she had let her imagination run riot as a little girl. Cat had learned the lesson well, she could hold herself together rigidly. It stood her in good stead now. She could cope with whatever came her way, she would deal with it as it arose. She would be calm and...

A branch cracked behind her.

Cat shot to her feet and spun around.

What...? Where...?

Something was coming through the forest!

There was a crackling, a crashing, steps coming nearer—Cat frantically cast about her for a stick, a stone, anything to defend herself with, but before she could reach the large branch that lay not five feet away from her, in the archway between the trees a small figure came into view.

Obviously alien, it stood no more than three feet high, and its skin, or fur, was a peculiar slippery-looking dark red. It tottered unstably on two leg-like appendages and waved one paw in front of its body. The other seemed to grow out of its facial orifice and lead from there to the side of its trunk. The creature stopped, tilted back its head, and looked at Catriona with two large, turquoise eyes.

CHAPTER 2

A LIENS. THIS PLACE WAS inhabited by small, red, humanoid aliens. Brilliant. Cat had seen too many sci-fi shows in which the cute, childlike aliens turned out to be vicious, sharp-fanged killers to be taken in by this one.

Wait—cute, and childlike?

Child-*like*?

She stared back at the turquoise-eyed creature, and suddenly all the alien features resolved into something entirely familiar and non-threatening: a human toddler, covered from head to foot in some sticky, dark-red substance, the fingers of its left hand firmly planted in its mouth.

The little person solemnly regarded Cat, then pulled its fingers out of its mouth, smacked its lips a few times, and stated: "Bubbafump."

Oh. Human it might be, or at least a semblance of it, but the locals apparently did not speak English, and Cat had no way of understanding what the child was saying. Stuck on an alien planet, and the Babel fish was broken.

Well, at least this was a sign that the insects-as-rulers theory had just been her overactive imagination. She put on her best library storytime face, pasted on a smile she did not feel, and brightly asked: "Yes? What did you say?"

The child tipped its head to the side, looked at Cat out of its big turquoise eyes, then turned around and toddled back in the direction it had come from.

"Wait!" Catriona called, "wait for me!" She slapped the last of the leaf mould off the seat of her skirt and hurried after the baby.

The child was toddling down a path, no more than a narrow beaten track. It looked around, caught sight of Cat, giggled, and took off in a tottering run, disappearing around a bend.

"Oh come on!" Cat said, speeding up. "You're just going to fall on your no— Oh!"

There on the ground, stretched out a full length across the path, was a body.

It seemed to be a man, his arms splayed out at his side, one leg bent at an odd angle, and he, too, was covered in that dark red slippery-looking stuff. Cat clapped her fingers to her mouth. Was that blood? He wasn't—dead? Please, no... Things were bad enough already without the horror of a corpse!

The baby stopped. "Bubbafump!" it said again, pointing at the body.

Oh thank goodness! There was a very slight rise and fall of the man's chest—he was breathing! Cat drew in a breath and heaved it back out in a sigh of relief.

But what was it she was smelling here? An image of the community arts centre in Greenward Falls flashed across Cat's memory. Arts, crafts...? She sniffed again. What was it...? The smell came from that big puddle next to the path. It was huge, ten or twelve feet across, probably more of a pit than a puddle, and it was full of—Oh, of course! Clay! The red stuff was clay! And both the baby and the man were completely covered in it, head to toe.

"How the dickens did you manage to do that to yourself?" Cat said to the baby.

"Bubba!" it replied, squatting down next to the man and batting at him with its sticky hands, "Bubba bubba bubba!" *Shlup shlup shlup* went its clay-covered hands against the man's clay-covered chest.

"I see," Cat said. Not that she did, but it seemed rude not to make conversation with the only other person in the vicinity who was conscious. "So what are we going to do now, munchkin?"

What they really needed here was a 911 call. Cat reached for her purse. Which wasn't there, of course. Drat!

Well, what would emergency medical people do in such a situation? Was it anything she could try to do herself?

She dimly remembered the first aid manual she had weeded from the reference section on her last day at the library. (Dewey Decimal number 616.02. Which was completely irrelevant at the moment.) There had been something about tourniquets, and CPR, the Kiss of Life... Oh goodness, she hoped it wouldn't come to that. Kissing aliens had not been part of the plan for her holiday... And who knew if the biology of these aliens even lent itself to doing regular human CPR...

Wait. Who said anything about aliens, anyway? Cat squatted down beside the man. Leaving aside the fact that he was completely coated in clay, he actually looked perfectly normal, humanly speaking. He had a sharp, slightly hooked nose and high cheekbones, longish hair and shortish beard, from what she could tell under all that clay (although the hair colour was anyone's guess), and there were the requisite number of fingers on his long, slender hands. Ditto for the toes of the one foot that was bare. The other had on some kind of pull-on shoe, like a moccasin.

Cat looked at that shoe. So, sure, the man definitely seemed human, but he wasn't dressed like a normal (meaning modern) person. It was hard to tell what his clothes were actually like; they didn't seem anything like the stuff Cat was used to, say a hoody or jeans, and she couldn't see any zippers or Velcro, not even a button. He had on some kind of simply cut long-sleeved shirt that was laced down the front, and plain straight-legged pants, both of them probably dull-coloured as anything bright would have shown through the clay in places.

"Bubba bubba," went the baby (*shlup shlup*).

"Does bubba mean daddy?" Cat guessed.

"Gah!"

"Quite," Cat said. What now? "We could see if your daddy has a pulse. That, I think, I can do." She reached for the man's wrist.

The baby stopped slapping his chest and looked up at Cat with its brilliant turquoise eyes.

"Gah."

"Mm-hm," Cat replied absently, searching with her fingertips for the pulse point. There, that was it. Now you were supposed to count it—something about so many beats per quarter-minute. She looked at her wrist to time it. And remembered that her watch was in the drawer of the bedside table of Nicky's spare room, because Cat had had enough of schedules and time pressure and she was on holiday... So much for taking the man's pulse. Not that she'd know what a healthy heart rate was, anyway. She randomly counted the beats for a little while anyway. They were regular and seemed reasonably strong, so the man was probably not in imminent danger of dying.

Cat laid his hand back on the ground and sat back on her heels, reflexively wiping her clay-smeared hand on her skirt. Oh no! A big streak of red clay ran across the blue stripe. And she'd got some on her blouse as well. Drat and double drat!

"Bibby?" suddenly came a voice through the forest. "Bibby! Babe? Where are you? Bibby?" Indubitably human, adult human at that, and female. "Bibby!" The voice came closer.

The baby scrabbled to its feet. "Ahn!" it cried, toddling away down the path.

A stocky woman came striding around the next bend, her greying hair pinned in a coronet on the top of her head, her long skirt multi-coloured and multi-tiered.

"There you are, child," she said as her eye fell on the baby. "Just look at you! Head to foot all over clay! What is your scatter-headed father about—ah!" She broke off as she caught sight of the body on the ground. "Now what has he done to himself?" She shook her head, her forehead wrinkled, then she looked up and saw Cat.

She stared at Cat for a moment, and abruptly her eyebrows rose as if she had had a surprise of recognition. "Hm!" she said. "And who might you be?"

Cat suddenly realized that she understood everything the woman said. Apparently the Babel fish had suddenly started working... Except she'd never had one of those in the first place. So did the locals speak English then? Or had being transplanted to their world made her understand their language as if it were her own?

The baby pointed at the man.

"Bubbafump!" it said to the woman.

"Yes, Bibby," said the woman, a trace of exasperation in her voice, "I can see that Papa went thump—again! What I really want to know is how, and what injuries he got himself this time." She pointed her chin at Cat. "Did you see what happened?"

Cat shook her head. "No, I'm sorry, I only just..."

"Ah, yes. You only just got here, didn't you. No need to apologize. Well then, time to deal with this young fool." She knelt down beside the man and lightly slapped his cheek. *Shlup, shlup.*

"Boy?" She lifted his eyelid briefly, then clicked her tongue. "Probably was going for more stuff," she said, tipping her head at a couple of metal buckets by the side of the path, one of them half-filled with clay. "And of course he couldn't wait until someone was there to look after the child, so he took her along. Never goes anywhere without her, the young fool." (Ah, so the baby was a girl?) "As to what happened to put them both into the state they're in, that's anyone's guess. She probably fell in the clay pit and he hauled her back out and slipped in the process. That leg doesn't look too good."

She lifted the man's twisted leg up and felt along the knee, then placed it back on the ground. Her hand came away stained a bright red, and Cat blinked. She had been very silly, hadn't she, to mistake the dull red-brown of the clay for blood.

"Nothing's broken," said the woman, raising the man's head and feeling along the back of it. "The main hurt looks to be the leg, and that's not bleeding so badly that we can't take him to his house before patching him up. Take his legs, I'll get him under the arms."

She slid her arm under the man's shoulders, hoisted him up against her, and stood up with a groan.

Take his legs? Okay. Cat stepped between the man's splayed legs, squatted down, and grabbed the calves. Slippery, muddy, squishy clay all over... With a wince, Cat tucked the legs against her sides and got to her feet. She barely caught herself from slipping in the thick layer of mud beneath the man's body (steadfastly refusing to think about her lovely suede ballerina flats that had been a pale beige only that morning), and looked across at the older woman. Who was almost a head shorter than Cat.

"Uh, ma'am..."

The woman raised an eyebrow. "Well?"

"Uh, it—it might work better if we switched... I—I don't know, but it might not be so good for his head to be lower than the rest of his body?"

"Of course." The woman gave a brief nod. "Put down the legs." She was a rather, umm, decisive person, wasn't she.

Cat gently lowered the man's legs back to the ground and stepped over his knee to get around to the head. Her blouse and skirt stuck to her side, clammy with clay, and with a wince she pulled her right sleeve away from her arm where there was a patch saturated with blood. And here she'd been worried about wiping her hand on her skirt.

Transferring the man from the woman's arms to Cat's proved to be a further difficult manoeuvre, and when she finally had him properly under the armpits, his muddy head lolled awkwardly and his arms dangled at his side, the hands drooping in the mud. That wasn't right either. Oh, for a proper ambulance stretcher...

But wait, that weeded-out first aid manual, there had been something in it about a more secure way to move an unconscious person. The Rautek grip, or some such thing? Cat closed her eyes to picture the illustration. Yes, that was it.

From under the man's arm, Cat fished for a grasp on his sleeve. She managed to grab a hold of the slippery fabric (this would be so much easier if there weren't so much clay everywhere!) and pulled his right forearm up across his chest. She grasped his wrist in her left hand, his forearm just below the elbow in her right and, using his arm across his chest like a holding bar, pulled him back firmly against herself, bringing his head to rest against her shoulder. She reached for his other sleeve, pulled this arm, too, across his chest, managed to lay it over the other arm, and had him in a firm hold without either head or arms dangling or dragging on the ground. Carefully, she raised herself to a standing position.

The woman looked at Cat with her eyebrows raised just a bit, then gave another one of her decisive nods. "It'll do," she said. She picked up the hem of her skirt, which nearly swept the ground, and bundled it into her waistband, exposing a pair of sturdy calves and feet encased in moccasins like the one the man still had on his foot. She turned her back to Cat, stepped between the man's legs, squatted down, picked them up around the knees, tucked them under her arms, and rose to her feet again.

"It's not the best thing for that wound," she said to Cat over her shoulder, "but needs must, we have to get him home. Come, Bibby!" She stepped sideways, turning them in the direction of the path, and with the little girl obediently toddling along behind them, they carried their unconscious burden legs first down the forest path.

CHAPTER 3

C AREFULLY STEPPING ALONG THE narrow path, they rounded a corner and emerged in a clearing. In front of them was a small house, whitewashed, with wooden shingles on the roof, a plank door in the centre, and two windows on either side of that. Attached to it on the right was another building, perhaps a small stable or a workshop; on the other side, a slat fence surrounded a tangle of growth that looked like a kitchen garden. It put Cat in mind of the open-air museum she had seen in Europe that had featured restored medieval cottages.

The determined woman steered them to the wooden door and pushed at it with her foot. It didn't open.

"Bibby, child, see if you can get that door."

The baby toddled around in front of her and tipped her head to the side.

"Doh?" she asked.

"Yes, dear, the door. Open it."

"Bibby doh," said the mud-covered little girl. She reached up to the door handle with both hands and pulled downwards; the door popped open and she fell into the house. "Waaaaah!"

"Oh child!" said the woman, clicking her tongue as they manoeuvred the man past the wailing baby, who was scrambling up with her round bottom sticking into the air. "It's all right, come, little one."

The room they had entered looked like it comprised the entire cottage. On the right-hand wall, some live coals glowed in a large, open fireplace; a door next to it led into the annex. Against the back wall stood a deal table with a chair on one end and a bench on either side, while on the left-hand side of the room, its headboard under the window, was a wooden platform bed covered in rumpled blankets and a multi-coloured quilt.

"Let's put him down here," said the woman over the wails of the baby, tipping her head towards the right side of the room. "The first thing to do is to clean him up." She steered them to the fireplace, used her foot to push aside a green-and-blue-striped hearth rug, and lowered the man's legs to the floor.

The bare floor? Ah well, it wasn't like he could get any dirtier. If anything, it was him who was dirtying the floor. And being unconscious, he wouldn't care how hard the floorboards were. Cat slowly lowered herself to one knee, slid her arms out from under his, caught his head in her hands, and gently laid it down. Phew! She rolled her shoulders and shook out her arms; the last hundred yards or so had been a challenge. He was no lightweight.

"There, there, little one," the woman said, scooping up the baby, "no need to carry on so." The wails instantly subsided. "You are a right mess, though, aren't you?" She pulled a handkerchief from her pocket and wiped off the light-coloured snail trails that the tears and snot had made on the mud-covered little face. "Not that that's done much good," she said with a rueful look between the now filthy handkerchief and the baby's still-clay-smeared face. She put the child back on the floor.

"Now then—" She looked at Cat. "What's your name, girl? I can't just keep calling you 'you'."

Cat felt herself blush a little. She should have introduced herself before now. "I'm sorry," she said, "it's Cat—Catriona, really." Somehow her full name seemed more fitting in this place or this time, whatever or whenever it was.

"Nothing to be sorry for." The woman gave her a brief smile. "Catriona it is then. Mine's Ouska, or you can call me Aunt, like he does." She pointed her chin at the man on the floor. "Let's get him cleaned up. Can you see if there's water in the bucket? Should be by the door." She vanished through the door beside the fireplace, only to reappear a minute later with an armful of rags and towels. "They're half of them smeared with clay anyway," she muttered. "Don't think he ever cleans up that stuff!"

Cat found an enamelled bucket half full of water next to the front door—it was a wonder the baby hadn't knocked it over when she tumbled into the house—and carried it over to the man on the floor. She eyed him rather dubiously. That was a lot of clay he was covered with, him and the baby both. Half a bucket of water wasn't going to do the job.

"No, it won't. We'll just have to make do for now," Ouska said, as if Cat had spoken aloud. She scooped up the baby who was toddling around the cottage, leaving muddy footprints all over the floor, and deposited her on the chair by the table. "You sit here and don't move, Bibby."

"Yit?" asked the baby.

"Yes, sit. And be good, just for a few minutes."

"Bibby yit," said the little girl.

"Good girl," the woman said, as she began to undo the laces on the man's shirt. "We'd better get the clothes off first," she said to Cat. "Here, you lift him, while I—yes, that's right."

The mess of getting the man cleaned up was phenomenal, and the embarrassment of it only marginally less so. Ouska grabbed a pair of shears from a shelf next to the door and unceremoniously slit the man's pants right up the side of the injured leg, then pulled them off. When Cat looked back around again, she found to her relief that he was wearing some kind of whitish drawstring boxer shorts by way of underwear. Thank goodness. Full frontal nudity would have been just one thing too many.

The older woman took one of the larger rags, soaked it in the bucket, then washed as much of the clay off the man as she could get. Within minutes the water in the bucket looked as murky as the clay pit itself.

"Hmph," Ouska said, looking at the bucket. "Know how to work a pump?"

"Uh—I don't know... I've used some at camp when I was a kid, but..."

"Never mind," the older woman said, her tone kind but brisk. "I keep forgetting you've come from quite another place. Yes, I know, we'll talk about that later. You're a bright girl, Catriona, you'll see how it works. The pump is outside on the side of the workshop. The handle creaks a lot, but you just need to work it a few times and it'll start. Don't overfill the bucket, we can't have you hurting yourself as well." She handed Cat the bucket with the remaining water and tipped her head in the direction of the door.

When Cat came back with the cleaned, filled bucket (the pump was indeed just like the ones they'd had at camp the summer Cat was twelve), Ouska had a large shallow pottery bowl on the floor beside the man's head and a jug in her hand.

"Let's try cleaning up his head at least a little bit," she said. "If you hold him up I'll pour." She dipped the jug into the bucket.

Cat got her arm under the man's neck and lifted his head; Ouska pushed the bowl under his head and poured water over his hair, trying to rinse out some of the clay. The hair and beard that emerged were red; Cat didn't think that was just the residue from the clay.

After just a few minutes of holding the man like this, her back was aching and her arm started to shake. He was slender, but his chest and arms were surprisingly muscular. Didn't they say muscle weighed more than fat?

"Ouska, I don't know if I can..."

The older woman shot her a look.

"Of course, child." She reached for a cloth and towelled off the man's hair. "There, you can put him down. Not the best, but it'll have to do, we can't give him a bath now."

"Bubbabaff!" said the little girl from her perch at the table. "Bibbybaff!"

"Yes, dear," said Ouska, "you'll get a bath soon. But first we have to see to Papa."

"Bubba leep!"

"Yes, Papa is asleep," the woman said absently, gently probing the injury on the side of the man's leg.

Asleep? That certainly wasn't what it looked like to Cat!

Ouska looked up at her, then smiled and gave a tiny shake of her head. "No, of course not. But it's better if she thinks so." She peered at the wound. "There's something stuck in this—a twig, a piece of wood, something hard like that. It's got to come out, or it'll fester." She rose to her feet. "I doubt he's got anything here to pull it out with; I'll have to get it from my house. Meantime, we'll wrap this up and get him to bed."

She went to the shelf by the door, took down a clean dish towel, and twisted it snugly around the leg. Then she pulled the quilt and most of the blankets off the bed. The one brown blanket that was left was woven of a coarse, brown material and sported several holes; she spread it over the mattress and pillow, clicking her tongue.

"Fit for nothing but a horse blanket, that is," she muttered. "Well, it won't matter if it's spoiled, that's for certain. Come on, Catriona, he'll be more easy on the bed."

They moved the man up on the bed, and Cat picked up another one of the blankets and laid it lightly over him.

He still had not recovered consciousness, but his breathing was relatively regular, and the fact that Ouska, who appeared to know what was what, didn't seem to be worrying about his being unconscious was reassuring to Cat.

"Very well, your turn, little one," the older woman said. She picked up the baby, made short shrift of stripping her of her clay-encrusted little tunic and the drawers she wore underneath (not, thank goodness, diapers—that would take the level of mess-es-to-be-dealt-with just a bit too far), and stood her right in the water bucket. The little girl squealed, and Ouska chuckled. "You've got to have your bath, dear," she said.

"Bibbybaff, Bibbybaff!" the baby chanted as she was rinsed from head to toe, then lifted out of the bucket, rubbed dry with one of the coarsely-woven towels that hung on a hook by the fire, and bundled into a clean set of drawers and a tunic which Ouska had pulled from a carved chest beside the bed. The little girl's hair was definitely red, and now that it was clean it clustered in soft, short ringlets all over her head.

Cat grabbed one of the rags that still had some dry spots on it and mopped up the water and excess clay from the floor, then used it to wipe down the chair and table where the baby had liberally coated whatever she could reach with mud. She got the worst of it off, but there was still a smear of clay over everything.

"Thank you, dear," Ouska said, gathering up the clay-soaked clothing and dirty rags and bundling them into the corner by the fireplace.

"It's not coming off, I don't think," Cat said, dunking her rag in the murky water in the bucket and wringing it out.

"One more bucket of clean water should help," Ouska said, "and then we'll leave the rest for tomorrow." She wiped at the seat of the chair with her mostly-clay-covered skirt and sat the baby back down.

When Cat came back in with another bucket of fresh water, she found a couple of candles lit on the mantelpiece, and Bibby sat at the table munching on a chunk of cheese and a piece of coarse bread (the kind that the specialty bakery in Greenward Falls called 'artisan bread'. Cat suspected that there wasn't anything 'artisan' about it here).

Ouska folded some of the blankets into a little pallet in the corner beside the table.

"The little one can sleep on here for tonight," she said. "The chamber pot is under the bed, and the privy is out back for when you need it or want to empty the pot." She walked over to the shelf next to the door, took down a jug, filled it with fresh water from the bucket, and set it on the table. "The water is quite good to drink, and there's the cheese and bread. I'll get back as soon as I can, but it might be some time. I'll try to—"

"Get back?" Cat interrupted. "Where are you going?" The woman couldn't leave her alone here, with an injured, unconscious man, and a tiny girl, and...

"Now, child," said the older woman soothingly, "don't fret yourself. I told you I need to get my tongs to get that stick out of that wound of his; there's nothing here to do a clean job with. Aside from that, it's getting on for dark, and I have things to see to that can't wait—the chickens and Uncle, for one. You'll do fine, girl. I'll hurry back, but even if I'm not here soon, I'm sure you can manage. You've got a good head on your shoulders."

No, not really. And even if it were true, how on earth would she know that?

The woman gave a chuckle. "I know things, Catriona, and this is one of them. So don't," she gave Cat a pointed look, "fret yourself."

She turned to the door, but suddenly stopped, swung around, and marched around the bed. She lifted the lid of the chest that she had taken little Bibby's clothes from, shuffled a few cloth items around until she reached the bottom, and pulled out some green and brown pieces.

"Here," she said, holding them out to Cat. "You need to get out of those muddy clothes. These should do you, they were his wife's, and you're much of a height and build. It's not like that woman will be needing them anymore."

Cat took the clothes from Ouska, holding them as far away from her own clay-and-blood-smeared ones as possible. (Would she ever get that outfit clean again?) "Thank you."

The older woman gave her a nod, then she turned to the bed, gazing down at the man. A soft look came into her eyes, and she laid the back of her hand on his forehead in an almost caressing gesture.

Then she shook herself. "Hmph," she said, turning around to look down at little Bibby crumbling bread on the surface of the table. For just a moment, she rested her hand on the baby's hair, which was drying into short red-blonde curls sticking out like feathers from a ruffled baby bird. The little girl smiled up at her. "Ahn!" she said.

Ouska gave Cat another one of those arrow-straight looks. "You'll do fine," she repeated, and walked out of the cottage into the dusk.

CHAPTER 4

C AT TOOK A DEEP breath. Okay. She was stuck in a cottage without power or running water, in a magical forest, with a tiny girl who didn't speak English (much), an unconscious injured man (she realized she didn't even know his name), and no cell phone to call 911 (not that there was likely to be a 911 service anyway), while the only person who seemed to know what was going on had disappeared, possibly never to come back.

Cat felt like something had her by the throat, squeezing it tight.

This was nuts! How bizarre a situation could you even be in? What crazy thing was going to happen next? She didn't even dare to—to—say, pick up that brown pottery cup from the table; for all she knew, it might just whirl her off into yet another dimension.

Come to think of it, being whirled off to someplace else might not be such a bad idea. The situation couldn't get much worse than the fix she was in right now, could it? Maybe the cup would take her back to the museum in Greenward Falls, you never could tell.

She dropped the clean clothes onto the bench by the table, snatched up the cup, held her breath, and stared fixedly into the depths of the vessel.

There was some dried-on milk in the bottom.

And nothing whatever happened.

"Gah?" said Bibby.

Cat sighed and looked up. It appeared that her attempt to hypnotize the pottery cup into transporting her back to twenty-first-century America was a failure—not that she'd held out much hope in the first place.

She put the cup back on the table. A corner of her mind took note of the fact that it was a really nice piece; it fit her hand perfectly and was just the right shape and weight to be pleasant to hold, with a lovely smooth lip. Whoever had made that cup knew what they were doing.

Cat drew a breath to loosen the tightness in her throat, then smiled at the baby, more to reassure herself than for the little girl's sake.

"Well, Little Bibby, it's you and me and your daddy, isn't it. I just hope he doesn't wake up, or die, or do anything else that I don't know what to do about."

The little girl climbed off the chair and toddled over to Cat.

"Gah!" She patted at the pile of clothes on the bench.

"Okay, you're right. I might as well." Cat picked up the clothes at arm's length—a skirt, tiered in earth-brown and dark green, and a tunic blouse in lighter brown—and turned around in a circle. Where could she change? There wasn't even a cupboard to hide behind. Ah, whatever.

It wasn't like a small child would care, and the man was unconscious.

Just the same, Cat turned her back to the bed, then slipped off her shoes—best not to look at them too closely—and took off her poor muddy and bloody blouse and skirt. There was no underwear with the new clothes, so she kept on her own. Her bra was kind of damp, but not too bad; with a clean shirt over top it should dry off.

She slipped the brown tunic over her head and laced it up at the neck; the skirt had a drawstring and came down to her ankles. They were actually quite comfortable—a nice soft fabric, and the fit was long and loose, but not too baggy, as Ouska had predicted. Cat gave a snort. What would Ryan say if he saw her now?

She draped her muddy, damp clothes over the bench to dry off; time enough to deal with them in the morning.

It was getting darker in the cottage as daylight faded outside, the candles on the mantelpiece would soon be the only illumination left. Cat was wondering how Ouska had lit them. She stood up on tiptoe and peered along the mantelshelf. Nothing that looked like matches or a lighter, unless that jar of sticks... No, they were just skewers. Maybe Ouska had used a tinderbox? That's what people used in places like this, wasn't it? But there wasn't one of those either as far as Cat could see. Not that she knew exactly what one would look like, or would know how to use it anyway.

Well, there was some light in the room now, and Cat just hoped the candles would last until Ouska got back. The woman did say she'd come back soon, didn't she?

All right, what now? Cat took a look around the cottage. She'd had hardly had any thought to spare for her surroundings up to now, what with all the commotion of looking after the man on the bed. Cat gave him a quick glance. He was still lying motionless, apart from his chest gently rising and falling with each breath.

Keep breathing, Cat thought at him, *just keep breathing!*

In the corner beside the bed, where the front door would hide it when it was open, stood what was surely a kind of chair. Ouska had piled the blankets on top of it, so it was hard to tell, but Cat could see the outline of a high back, and a part of a carved armrest was showing.

Cat scooped up the pile of blankets, and gasped in surprise.

It was a rocking chair, a fantastically beautiful piece, utterly unlike the plain simplicity of the other furniture in the cottage. Fashioned from a dark, shining wood (black walnut, perhaps, if they had walnuts in this place), the high back and the sides supporting the arm rests were pierced and carved in an intricate pattern. Cat could make out roses, lilies, daffodils, and honeysuckle twining up the sides, curving around the top, and winding themselves in a riot of blossoms and vines around a medallion in the centre of the back. The small oval held a bird, a tiny songbird with its beak open in a cheerful melody, the bright eyes and tilt of the head reminding Cat of nothing so much as of Bibby's little face. In fact, the bird *was* Bibby.

"Dair!" said the little girl, who had toddled over and stood clutching Cat's skirt.

"Yes, that's some chair all right!" Cat ran her hand over the baby's head—such soft curls!—and looked back at the rocker. Taking the blankets off the chair had set it very gently in motion, swaying back and forth. It looked so cozy, so inviting... It was almost like it was pulling at her...

Bibby let go of Cat's skirt and patted the polished, smoothly curved seat.

"Dair. Yit," she commanded.

"Mmm, yes, sit..." Cat said. That sounded so wonderful. That was exactly what she wanted, to sit in that chair and let it soothe the kinks out of her back, let her rest, calm her soul...

But first she had to deal with that armful of blankets. She carried them over to the other side of the bed (the man was still softly breathing), and dumped them on top of the chest against the wall. Being across the room from the chair, its pull seemed to have lessened just a bit. She still wanted to go sit down in it, but perhaps there were a few other things to do first.

"Just wait a few minutes, okay? We'll sit in the chair really soon," she told the little girl. She tore a chunk off the bread and broke a piece off the cheese that were still on the table, then wrapped the rest in the waxy sort of cloth they sat on (wasn't that called oil cloth?) and carried it over to the shelves under the window next to the door. There were some stacked brown pottery dishes, plates and bowls and cups (like the one that had failed to transport Cat back to America), and an unglazed earthenware jug with a cloth draped over it that stood in a dish of water. She tucked the bread-and-cheese bundle between that and a covered jar with a wooden handle sticking out of a notch in the lid; it looked like the honey pots sold by the beekeeper at the farmer's market in Greenward Falls.

The not-artisan bread turned out to be chewy and nutty, the cheese sharp and crumbly. It wasn't until she took the first bite that Cat realized how hungry she was. When was the last time she'd eaten? She had been planning to have lunch with Nicky after looking at the museum, but then... So her last meal had been breakfast. But did time pass at the same rate here (wherever "here" was) as it did at home (wherever, for that matter, "home" was at the moment)? Was breakfast as far back as it would have been there, or a much longer, or shorter, time ago?

Cat gave a little shudder. It was all so surreal, she couldn't even handle thinking about it. The bread and cheese hit the spot, though, and now that the hollow feeling in her belly had abated, she realized she needed the bathroom rather badly. Ouska said something about a privy, outside? Or "out back," she'd actually said.

There was barely enough light outside to see by now, but Cat did find the privy, clear around the back of the house, in the corner where the side building jutted out a bit further than the house. It was an outhouse just like the ones on the campground she'd been to with Nicky last summer, built of wooden slats, with a bench seat with a hole that was covered with a giant wooden lid when it wasn't in use. No toilet paper—or maybe she just couldn't see any, in the dark. And of course no sink to wash your hands.

Cat made do with rinsing off her hands under the pump, shook the last drops of water from her fingers, and dried the rest on her skirt. When she stepped back into the house, night had fallen outside; the candles cast soft globes of a yellow glow into the darkness. Bibby had climbed into the rocking chair and sat quietly with her thumb in her mouth. Her eyelids were drooping over those big turquoise eyes; she raised one little fist and rubbed at her eye.

What a cutie. Better get her to bed.

Oh, but the baby wasn't wearing a diaper, she'd have to go to the bathroom, too! And Cat wasn't about to take her out in the dark to the outhouse and have her fall into that hole. Oh dear. This was all so complicated.

Cat had done some babysitting in her teens. Sure, that was almost ten years ago, but things came back to you, didn't they? Or so she'd read. Hopefully her child care skills were among those things-that-come-back.

She picked up little Bibby from the rocking chair, leaving it softly swaying behind her, and stood the little girl on the floor. Yes, she still knew how to pick up a toddler. Now, how did little kids go to the bathroom?

Ah, but hadn't Ouska said something about a chamber pot? In other words, a potty? That sounded like the thing to use. Under the bed, if Cat remembered correctly. Yes, there it was, a large pot-bellied bowl with a handle on one side and a pouring spout on the other. A pouring spout? Cat made a face. But you had to dump the stuff somehow, so she supposed it made sense. And come to think of it, she had seen chamber pots like this in pictures, and even once, she remembered now, in a museum. Rather like this one, except there it had been white, and enamelled, not brown pottery. But then this one had a lid, which was a bonus.

Very well. "Go potty, Bibby?" she asked in a high-pitched voice. Good grief, why was she talking like this? Silly. "Do you need to go potty, Bibby?" she repeated in a more normal tone.

"Bo-be," said the baby sleepily, and tugged at her tunic. Her underpants were a simple drawstring affair, easy enough to slip down (thank goodness). Cat made use of one of the rags to wipe the little girl's bottom and pulled up the drawers again. She'd have to figure out what they used for toilet paper around here soon, else she'd have to steal a few more of those rags for the privy, and there weren't any left that were clean enough for even that purpose.

The little girl was barely able to keep her eyes open anymore; her head was beginning to nod and she was knuckling both her eyes now. "Nigh-nigh..." she said softly and sleepily.

Cat pulled back the blanket on the top of the little pallet, then picked up the baby and laid her down on it. She knelt on the floor beside the makeshift bed, tucked the blanket around the little girl's shoulders, and gently stroked the soft hair.

"Good night, sweetie," she said. Bibby had her thumb in her mouth, and her long eyelashes lay fanned out on her cheeks. Deep breaths showed that she was already most of the way to dreamland.

Cat smiled down at the baby, then she sat back onto her heels.

Now what?

It was completely dark, except for the little globes of light the candles cast around them. The rocking chair across the room still exercised that mysterious pull on her, and at any rate, there was nothing to do now but wait.

Cat fished a blanket out of the pile on the chest and wrapped it around herself; it was some kind of woolly material, softer than it looked. She walked around the bed with the quietly breathing man on it, and sank back into the rocking chair.

An involuntary sigh of relief escaped her. That was the most comfortable chair she had ever sat in. She couldn't even feel the carving in the back rest, and it cradled her like a smooth, comforting hug, swaying gently back and forth.

Cat leaned back her head against the back rest, and softly rocked to the rhythm of the breathing of the man and the little girl.

CHAPTER 5

An HOUR OR TWO later, Cat was startled awake. The man on the bed was muttering and moving around. Restlessly he tossed his head from side to side, his breathing ragged and uneven.

Cat sprang to her feet.

What to do?

If only she'd gone into nursing, not library work... Then again, how was she meant to have known that she'd be left to look after an injured man in a strange quasi-medieval magical place without even a first-aid kit to help her out? Come to think of it, modern medical training probably wouldn't have been much help here, either—the lack of a first-aid kit was one of the clues.

She stepped over to the bed and looked down at the fretful man. He had tossed most of his covers off, exposing half of his chest, and his feet were tangled in the blanket. It looked quite uncomfortable.

Gingerly Cat reached out to pull the blanket back over him. This was embarrassing... Her fingers made contact with his bare skin, and quickly she snatched them back.

He was burning hot! No wonder he was tossing around so. He must have developed a fever from his injury.

Where was the bossy woman when you needed her?

Cat desperately tried to penetrate the darkness beyond the window with her gaze, willing Ouska to come back. But there was nothing. All she could see in the window panes was the reflection of the candles on the mantelpiece, now more than half burned down.

The man moaned.

There was nothing else for it, Cat had to try to do something for him on her own. People used to sponge feverish patients with cool water, didn't they? At least that's what Victorian novels would have you do. Along with giving the sick person calf's foot jelly and strengthening broths. Not that she had any of those on hand, nor a sponge, for that matter. She wasn't even sure what calf's foot jelly was, exactly. The best she could do right now was to untangle his covers and hope it would make him a bit easier.

Cat gently pulled the blanket free, careful not to touch the injury, and straightened it out over the man's feet.

He was twisting his head from side to side, his hands snatching at the blanket, at his arms, at nothing. She reached for the top edge of the blanket to pull up over his chest.

And suddenly found her wrist clamped in an iron grip.

Startled, her gaze flew to the man's face. His eyes were wide open, staring. Turquoise again—even in the dim candlelight Cat could make out the colour. He looked at her with a glassy gaze that told Cat he wasn't really seeing her, but his grasp on her wrist was hard, unyielding.

"It's okay, you're all right," she murmured at him, "don't worry, you'll be fine." The soothing noises came out almost automatically; it wasn't as if she had any idea if he was, in fact, all right and would be fine.

She tried to pry his fingers off her arm, not breaking eye contact. After a long minute, his glassy stare wavered. He blinked, and his grip loosened just a little. Cat managed to unclasp the hot fingers from around her wrist, but when she tried to pull free he grasped again, this time catching her hand and holding it tight.

"Karana!" His voice was rough, raspy. "Karana—marry me!"

What?!?

Now this was getting ridiculous. Cat tried to pull her hand away. No way was she going to agree to marry a total stranger, in a strange place, who wasn't even conscious of what he was saying...

Wait. He wasn't conscious of what he was saying. He didn't know who she was; he thought she was this Karana person, whoever that was. Maybe agreeing with him would calm him down enough to settle him again for a little while.

"Karana!" he insisted, his scratchy voice pleading. His eyes were deeply worried, the brows contracted with pain and emotion.

Very well. You had to humour sick people, didn't you?

"Karana..."

"Yes," Cat said, gently laying her free hand over the fingers that clutched her. "Yes, I'll marry you."

He heaved a deep sigh, and the worried look drained from his turquoise eyes.

A soft whimper came from the corner of the room. Bibby! The whimper grew louder and became a full-blown cry. The man frowned, and he twisted his head on the pillow, searching for the sound.

"It's all right, I'll get her," Cat said. The clutching fingers let go of her, and she gently laid his hand down on the covers, pulled the blanket up over his chest, and stood up to deal with the baby.

Bibby, too, had kicked off her blanket, and her little legs were icy cold.

"There, there," Cat said, scooping the little girl up in her arms. Thank goodness the baby hadn't wet her pants. Cat carried her back to the rocking chair, fished with her foot for the blanket she had dropped on the floor, managed to hook it with her toes, and balanced on one foot so she could grab a corner of it. She wrapped it around herself and Bibby to keep out the chill that had settled on the cottage, then sank back into the chair and began rocking.

A glance at the man on the bed showed that his eyes were closed again and he was lying still, but his posture was tense, and his forehead furrowed in pain.

Bibby had stopped crying when Cat picked her up, but she was still giving short, sobbing breaths and making little whimpery noises. Cat hugged the little body to herself, trying to infuse it with her own warmth. Bibby snuggled close and sniffled.

"Shh, baby, shh," murmured Cat (sway back, and forth, back, and forth), "shh, baby..."

The man on the bed stirred again, twisting his head left and right with a jerky motion.

"Shh, baby..." Cat hummed (sway back, and forth, back, and forth...). Her hum turned into a melody, slow, gentle, one note up, one note down. "Humm, huhh, humm, huhh..."

The hum became a lullaby.

"Sleep, my child, and peace attend thee
All through the night,
Guardian angels God will lend thee,
All through the night..." (sway back, and forth, back, and forth...)

The whimpering in Cat's arms grew quieter; the twisting on the bed slowed.

"Soft the drowsy hours are creeping, (back, and forth, back, and forth)

Hill and dale in slumber steeping, (back, and forth)

Love alone his watch is keeping, (back, and forth, back, and forth)

All through the night..."

The baby gave a big sigh, put her thumb in her mouth, and snuggled deeper into Cat's arms. The man's body relaxed, and he drew slow, quiet breaths.

Cat leaned back her head; the rocking chair cradled her and the baby (softly, gently swaying back, and forth). Her song became a hum, then a whisper.

One of the candles on the mantel guttered and went out; the other burned on with a steady yellow glow into the night.

CHAPTER 6

T HE DOOR LATCH RATTLED, and the wooden door creaked open. Cat slowly opened her eyes; they felt like they had sandpaper stuck to the inside of the lids. Cold dawn light filtered into the room. Had she been asleep? She must have been—her arms certainly still were. Little Bibby felt heavy on Cat's lap. Her thumb had slipped out of her mouth, a little bit of drool trickled down her cheek, and she was snoring a small baby snore.

Ouska stepped into the room and softly shut the door behind her.

"Here, let me take the little one," she said in a quiet voice, lifting the baby out of Cat's arms. She carried her back to her pallet on the other side of the room and tucked the blankets in around her.

Cat shivered in the chill of the room. The fire had gone out, the candles long burnt down. Her neck was stiff and sore, her fingers such lifeless sausages that they were useless for massaging the kinks out of it. She opened and closed her fists, trying to speed up the process of getting sensation back into her hands, then gave a little yelp and shook them hard as the pins and needles began to prickle all over them. That rocking chair might be the most comfortable piece of furniture Cat had ever sat in, but it was clearly not designed for sleeping in a whole night. She groaned.

So did the man on the bed. With a rush, the midnight events flooded back into Cat's memory.

"What happened between you two?" asked Ouska.

"No-nothing!" Now where had the woman got the idea that something had happened? Nothing had happened, nothing! Only a sick man's delirium, and a confused traveller's attempts to calm him. Cat felt herself blushing. Nothing at all.

"Oh? Doesn't feel like 'nothing' to me in here." The woman *was* a mind reader! "But never mind that now. If you can move again, we'll get on with this. He looks like he's taken bad."

"Yes. He woke up, sort of, in the night," (*stop blushing!*) "but I don't think he was really conscious. And he was really hot, and restless, and..."

"And you got him quiet again?" Ouska gave Cat a searching look. "And the babe, too. Well done."

Now why should this praise from a woman she hardly knew make Cat feel so absurdly proud?

Ouska laid her hand on the man's forehead and started back.

"Oh dear, he's bad. Let's look to that wound, and we'll see from there."

She pulled the blanket away from the injured leg and unwrapped the cloth from around the knee. The wound looked inflamed and sore.

"Hmm, the light isn't very good yet, but we'll have to make do. The sooner we get this done the better. I don't like the look of him." She took a small pair of iron tongs and some clean cloths out of her satchel. "Now, Catriona. I need you ready to hold him if he wakes or moves. Can you do that?"

"I—I think so," said Cat, hesitantly.

"Of course you can. Well, here we go."

At the first touch of the tongs, the man started up with a cry. Cat lunged across his body, reaching to hold down his leg, but Ouska already had a firm grasp on his shin with her left hand, her right wielding the tool.

The man's hands were flailing, wildly grasping at nothing. Cat caught his right hand in both of hers, and her touch seemed to give him focus. His eyes opened, staring at her without seeing; his fingers wrapped around hers, squeezing convulsively.

Cat clenched her teeth, hissing in a breath. That hurt! Suddenly he gave a scream, his grip became a crushing vice—then it went slack and his head fell back on the pillow. Unconscious again, thank goodness.

"Got it," Ouska said in a satisfied tone.

Through the tears that had shot into her eyes Cat saw that the older woman was holding up the tongs, a viciously sharp-looking piece of stick gripped in the points.

"What is that?" Cat wiped the tears from her eyes with the back of her left hand.

"Not certain. I have an inkling." Ouska tucked the little stick into the folds of a small white cloth and put it away in her satchel, then she took the lid off a round tin.

Cat smelled something familiar. Something like—Italian food?

"What are you doing?" she said, sniffling a bit and nursing her crushed hand against herself.

"Ointment of garlic and basilicum," Ouska said briefly, applying the cream to the wound on the leg.

"Oh!" Garlic and basil, no wonder it made Cat think of pesto. She remembered reading about those. "They're good against infections, aren't they?"

"Right. I hope we can keep it from getting worse—it's already gone a ways," the older woman said, wrapping a clean bandage around the wound. "Now that piece of wood is out, I think we have a chance." She gave Cat a searching look. "But what's he done to you? Got a grip on your hand, did he?"

Cat just nodded, biting her lip to keep the tears from starting up again.

"Hmph. Not what you needed just now. But it helped at that moment, or he would have kept me from doing what I had to. Here, girl, let me see." Ouska held out her brown, work-worn hand across the bed, and Cat laid her hurting hand on the palm. The older woman gently rubbed her thumb across the bruised joints, then she reached for her satchel.

"You've got no bones broken," she said, "although that wasn't a given with the strength the boy's got in his hands. Come here." She patted the edge of the bed next to her and opened yet another jar.

Cat walked around the bed and sat down next to Ouska, who spread some salve on a cloth and tied it around Cat's hands. "Comfrey ointment, should keep it from bruising too much," she said. "I know you hurt, and I'm sorry for it, but you'll do." She packed up her tools in the satchel again, then briskly got to her feet.

"Ouska? What... what happens now?"

"Now we wait. The next few hours should tell. But I doubt it will go poorly with him in the end; in spite of it all, there's something right about all of this. It has a lot to do with your being here, I know."

Being here... "Ouska—Ouska, where *am* I? What is this place? I don't even know what I'm doing here, what happened..." Cat swallowed hard past the lump in her throat, blinking to keep the tears from spilling out. It was really all too much.

The older woman gave her a long, kindly look.

"No, I don't suppose you do, do you? Very well," she said. "I think it's time we had a talk."

CHAPTER 7

OUSKA GLANCED DOWN ON the sleeping little girl on the pallet.

"It's a mercy she didn't wake up through all this," she said. "Babes can sleep through anything sometimes, and other times they wake at the slightest thing. And with her sense for people..." She reached for her satchel and took out a brown stoppered pottery flask, then went to the shelf and took down two of the cups. "Make yourself comfortable, Catriona, if you can stand that rocking chair again." She poured a small amount of a dark amber liquid into one of the cups.

Cat wrapped herself in the woollen blanket. Her feet were freezing from being barefoot on the wooden floor most of the night, so she settled herself into the rocking chair, tucked them under her, and awkwardly tried to stuff the blanket in around the edges with her left hand. Surprisingly, the rocker felt quite as comfortable on her back as the first time she sat down in it; her body seemed to have forgiven it for being stuck in it all night long.

"This'll warm you," said Ouska, putting the cup in Cat's hand. The drink smelled of apples, sharp and very alcoholic.

"What is it?"

"Applejack." The older woman brought over the kitchen chair to the foot of the bed and sat down with a cup of the drink for herself. "Careful, though, it's strong."

Cat took a cautious sip and nearly choked. That was hard stuff! The drink burned its way down her throat, then a lovely warmth spread through her body. The lump in Cat's throat dissolved, and even her toes no longer felt icy.

"Hmm, good!" she said, surprised, and ventured another sip.

The woman smiled. "Like I said, girl, take it easy. Uncle's applejack has clout, more than most. But then, you're not one to get drunk, are you? And you can use the warmth."

"Okay." Cat squared her shoulders resolutely. She was getting tired of being told by this woman who or what she was and what she did or did not do or feel. Never mind that Ouska was right on every count. "How do you know all that?"

Ouska's lips twitched, and Cat guessed, slightly annoyed, that she knew exactly what Cat was thinking.

"It's nothing to do with you, particularly; I'm an Unissima. So was that wife of his," she pointed her chin at the man on the bed, "but she misused it, more fool her. I think perhaps you are, too?"

"An Ooni-what?"

53

"Unissima. Only daughter of an only daughter. We have the Knowing. Don't they have that where you come from?"

"That's another thing—where I come from. More to the point, where did I get to? What is this place? It's not England in 1066 or something, is it?"

"Is that what your home is called, Ingaland? No, this is the Wald of Ruph, in Samach."

"Samack. That's the country? Or the town? Or the world? Or the, I don't know, universe? And what is this 'Wald' thing? Or this 'Roof' thing?" *You're starting to sound hysterical, Cat.*

There was a distinctly soothing note in Ouska's voice as she replied. "We're in the Wald—the forest—of Ruph, in the county of Samach. Ruph is the name of the village. We're the most remote county, a bit cut off from the rest of Isachang—that's our country—but we manage quite well on our own." She took a sip from her cup. "So, what did happen to you, girl? How did you come here?"

"Well, there was this bowl—no, there was this guy—well, it's all because of my boyfriend, really!"

Ouska raised her eyebrows, but she just gave a little nod for Cat to continue.

Cat fortified herself with another sip from her cup, letting the applejack burn down her throat before she spoke again.

"Ryan—that's my boyfriend—*was* my boyfriend—we'd been going out for almost half a year. Nicky (Monica, really, she's my best friend), she always said he was a rat. Well, she didn't *say* so, not at first, but she never liked him, I knew that—you can tell, can't you? But I didn't want to listen to her. I mean, she's had, I don't know, half a dozen boyfriends in the last few years alone; she's fun, and pretty (not like me), and those guys at her medieval re-enactors group fall for her in droves. And then there's me. Ryan was the only man who was interested in me in years.

"Turns out he only asked me out in the first place because he thought I was something important. We met at a Chamber of Commerce meeting; I was there representing the library in organizing the carnival, which is a big deal in Greenward Falls. He just moved to town; he had ambitions to make big money and figured the big-fish-in-a-small-pond thing would do the trick, and that being connected with someone 'in an official capacity' would help with that. But once he clued in to how unimportant an assistant librarian really is in that town, I suppose he kept me on a string because he thought I'd become head librarian soon and I'd be influential then. Good grief, as if I'd want to take Joan's job away from her! She won't be retiring for years." Cat had almost forgotten whom she was talking to; the words spilled out like a dam had burst.

"Anyway, so eventually it dawned on dear Ryan that I wasn't who he thought I was—really, he said so. Verbatim." She lowered her voice to a mock male timbre. "'I thought you were more success-minded and had some ambition!' Well, not in the way he wanted me to be, I'm not. So he dumped me.

"I probably shouldn't have taken it so hard, but then again, maybe it was just as well. Really, that was the last straw, it kind of pushed me over the edge. I mean, I liked my job well enough—I love being a librarian—but I've been in this position for six years, and I was just fed up with my life, with everything. So I—well, I quit. All of it. Handed in my resignation, gave notice on my apartment, got rid of the furniture, packed the rest of my stuff in boxes, and put them in Nicky's spare bedroom.

"I was going to get a ticket to somewhere new, and different, and exciting—I dunno, San Francisco, New York, Timbuktu—and then start over after that. Except that I didn't really have any place I wanted to go to in particular, and someplace new, well, it's kind of scary, isn't it?

"Yeah, I know, the joke's on me.

"So then today—no, yesterday—I was meant to meet up with Nicky at the museum downtown, the Sammelhauser, after she got off work. I've lived in Greenward Falls for six and a half years, and I've never actually been inside the place. Nicky was always hassling me about it. We were supposed to check out the exhibits, and have coffee, and then maybe go to some travel agency or something and look at brochures and then go home to her place and book my flight to exotic destinations.

"Except when I got to the museum, there was this bowl, and I looked at it and everything went swirly and weird, and then..."

Ouska, who had listened to Cat's recital without interruption, sat up at this.

"What was it like, this bowl?"

"Well, it was pottery, about so big"—Cat gestured with her hands—"kind of straight up and then curved in at the

56

top. The most amazing colour; I've never seen any other glaze like that. A bit like that Chinese pottery, I think the colour is called celadon; but this was much more vibrant, deeper—like their eyes, Bibby's and—and his." She looked at the man on the bed. "What's his name, anyway?"

"We call him Guy," replied the older woman.

As if he had heard his name, the man stirred and drew a laboured breath. Ouska put down her cup and leaned forward to touch his hand.

"Hmm," she said, "seems a little better; that's good. But it means we'll need some help here. Thank you for telling me your story, Catriona, you've come at the right time. Think you can cope with things here for another hour or so? I'm going to get Uncle."

CHAPTER 8

T HE DOOR CLOSED BEHIND Ouska, and Cat leaned
her head back in the rocking chair. The lovely
warmth from the applejack was dissipating slowly from
her body, but Ouska had relit the fire in the fireplace and it
was gradually taking the chill off the cottage. The sun had
come up and was sending a few rays through the trees outside into the room. The man on the bed—Guy?—drew
softly rasping breaths.

Cat let the events of the last eighteen hours drift
through her mind. She certainly hadn't bargained on
any of this, would never have believed any such thing
could happen. Unlike Nicky, who believed in all sorts of
things—fairies and elves and auras and crystals and the
power of dreams—Cat had always been the rational one.
Well, to be honest, Cat doubted that even Nicky really
believed in any of that, but she did a great job pretending.
It was one of the things that made her friend so attractive,
that childlike enthusiasm. Of course, the bushy head of
golden hair and Pocket Venus figure didn't hurt either, nor
for that matter the blue eyes that she'd open really wide

to gaze up at the other person as if they were the most fascinating sight she'd ever seen. And she wasn't putting it on; Nicky was genuinely interested in people. It seemed to attract them like iron filings to a magnet, especially the male variety. Cat had watched more than one guy fall under that spell and trail Nicky for days, until she either made it clear to him (in the nicest way possible) that he needed to pack up and leave, or else took pity on him and elevated him to official boyfriend status for a month or two. They never lasted longer than that; in spite of all her romantic entanglements, Nicky hadn't found what she was looking for in a man any more than Cat had. The only difference was that she had a wider field to pick from.

Cat sighed. She was so different from her friend. Even outwardly, she was boring—average height, average size, average brown hair, average brown eyes. Average, boring interests and skills, no special experience, no special degrees. Just an average boring bachelor's in English, with a boring career in librarianship. The only thing more boring would be a career as chartered accountant. Or banking; she imagined banking would be quite boring...

Cat's mind snapped back to the present, and her gaze went to the man on the bed. Something was different!

She reached out and felt his forehead. It was much cooler to the touch now, and beads of sweat were forming along his hairline. That was good, wasn't it? It meant that the fever had broken, if she remembered correctly (who would have thought that reading Victorian novels could come in so handy?). She had no idea if it was normal for a fever to form so quickly and then break so fast, but perhaps people's health issues were different here than they were at home.

At home... Did she *have* a home? Would she ever go back to Greenward Falls—and if so, was that home? She had wanted to leave, wanted adventure—and here she'd gotten it, with a vengeance. Be careful what you wish for...

Across the room, the baby made a deep sighing sound, wiggled, then sat up on her bed and rubbed her little fists in her eyes. Her feathery red curls stood out all over her head like a human dust mop, and her cheeks were flushed pink from sleep. She blinked her turquoise eyes (what an amazing colour that was!) and looked around until she found Cat. A big smile broke out on her face.

"Gah!" she said, scrambling to her feet.

Cat smiled back at her. "Good morning to you too, little sleepyhead!" She crossed the room and tried to pick her up, but with a little yelp at the pain in her hand she gave up on that and instead knelt to give the little girl a hug. "And how are you this morning?"

"Bubba!" said the baby, wiggling out of Cat's arms and toddling over to the bed.

"No, wait, Daddy's sleeping!" began Cat, turning around to stop her, but she suddenly found herself looking straight into that other pair of turquoise eyes.

Guy's brows were drawn together in a puzzled frown as he looked at Cat. His gaze slid away from her, sweeping around the room, then it came to rest on the little girl who was climbing up on the bed, and his eyes cleared.

"Bi...bby, Karana," he said weakly, his voice rough. He tried to pull his arm out from under the blanket to reach for the baby.

Karana? Wasn't—wasn't that what he had called Cat in the night? What she had assumed to be the name of another woman? Oh dear.

"Bubba bubba bubba!" sang the little girl happily, patting him on chest.

"Careful, sweetie, you'll hurt Daddy!" said Cat. She tried to scoop up the girl with one arm to get her off the bed. The man's eyes turned back to her, and the puzzled frown returned.

"Who... who you?" he asked in a slurred voice.

"Gah!" said Bibby, just as Cat was about to tell him. Cat gave her a surprised look. Did she know Cat's name? Was that what she meant by that word? Cat had assumed it was just random baby talk. She filed it away among all the other matters she needed to ask Ouska about.

"Yes, I'm Cat. Catriona, really. I found you in the woods, or rather, Bibby found *me*, and took me to you, and then Ouska came, and..."

He looked no less confused.

"Never mind," Cat said quickly. "I'm Cat, that's all."

"Oh," he said, then winced as he tried to move. "Wha'—wha' happen?"

"I don't really know. You were covered in mud—clay—and so was Bibby, and you've hurt your leg, I don't know how. Ouska patched you up some, and she's coming back, with your uncle, I think?" *You're babbling, Cat.* Now that he was properly awake and conscious, she felt acutely embarrassed at being in a stranger's bed-room, a male stranger at that. His eyes were becoming clearer as he looked around the room and then again scanned her face, seemingly trying to understand, to remember.

"I—I cannot..." He tried to clear his throat.

"No, never mind," Cat repeated, turning away from his probing gaze. Her eye fell on the cloths that Ouska had left behind on the clothes chest.

"Here," she said, "let me..." Awkwardly, with her left hand, she dabbed at his forehead, which was glistening with sweat.

"Thank ... you," he said quietly.

"Bibby do!" The little girl caught up a cloth and bat-ted it at her father's face.

"No, no, it's all right!" Cat laughed, trying to ward off the baby with her bandaged right hand.

"What ... happened ... to your ... hand?"

What happened...? *Oh my.* A hysterical little giggle forced its way out of Cat's throat, turned into a hiccup of laughter, and then the dam burst. She laughed and laughed, the pent-up tension, confusion, fear, and panic of the last hours escaping like steam from a safety valve.

Guy smiled, bewildered, but Bibby squealed with glee and slapped the bed with both her little hands.

"I'm sorry," gasped Cat, when she could draw breath. "I'm sorry—it's just that—what happened to my hand? *You* happened to it!"

"I did that?" He frowned in confusion. "Hold—were you—did I..."

"Yes, but never mind. You didn't know what you were doing."

"I'm sorry," he said quietly, obviously deeply chagrined. "May I..." He struggled to pull his hand from under the covers and stretched it out shakily to Cat.

"Oh! I..." Hesitantly, Cat laid her bandaged hand on his.

"I'm so sorry," he repeated, and gently placed his other hand on top. His hands were trembling with weakness, but she could feel his warmth through the cloth wrapped around her bruises.

Something happened, something she could not explain. It felt as though his touch drew away the pain, knit together what had been damaged.

Startled, Cat looked into Guy's face, but his eyes had closed, and his forehead furrowed again.

The door opened.

"Where is that fool of a nephew of mine?" called a hearty male voice.

"Unca!" Bibby threw herself at the stocky man who entered the room, Ouska right behind him.

CHAPTER 9

C AT WAS WALKING ALONG the forest path after Ouska, who carried little Bibby. They had left Guy with his uncle, along with buckets of water, soap, towels, medicines, bandages, and a pot of rather delicious-smelling soup.

"They'll do," Ouska had said as she picked up the baby. "And you look like you might want a wash yourself, Catriona. Come on, there's warm water at my house."

Warm water? That sounded heavenly.

So here Cat was, hurrying after the older woman. The borrowed skirt she wore was longer than her blue and green hippie skirt from home; it came right down to her ankles, so she held it clutched in her left hand, trying to raise the hem. She kept feeling like she would trip on it, and she needed to see where she was putting her feet.

Cat could feel every rock and protruding root through the soles of her ballerina flats. Dirty though they were, she'd had to put them on again; there weren't any shoes that fit her in that leftover collection of Guy's wife's clothes.

She wondered what had happened to that woman. Had she died? But Ouska didn't seem to have much respect for her memory, judging by her tone of voice every time she spoke of her, and from what Cat had seen of the older woman so far, if there had been a sad (let alone tragic) death, she'd be compassionate, not brusque.

After a few minutes walking, the forest path widened and smoothed out, and Cat dropped the hem of her skirt and hurried ahead to walk next to Ouska.

"So," she said, "you started telling me, but I've already forgotten. The forest is called—what, Roos?"

"Ruph. The Wald of Ruph. The village is called that too. The county is Samach, the country Isachang." Ouska shifted the toddler to her other hip. "When you came, did you stop right by the clay pit?"

"No, a bit further back and around the corner, deeper in the forest. There was a little clearing and some kind of enclosure, like a cage made of tree branches, but I didn't really look at it. I was too freaked out." It was odd that she could speak with the people in this place the way she would talk at home, back in twenty-first-century America. Somehow, with the rustic surroundings and the way they were dressed, you'd expect them to be talking in "thee's" and "thou's". Or perhaps they *were* using all that fancy language, and she just heard them as if they talked ordinary modern English? Maybe the air in this place had built-in translators. Babel fish air.

"Ouska?"

"Yes, child?" Cat was twenty-eight—hardly a child. But somehow she didn't mind Ouska calling her that. It didn't seem condescending, and it made her feel like here was someone who cared about her and wouldn't leave her hanging. Besides, it was better than being called "young fool" like Guy.

"Ouska—" (now, how could she put this question?) "Ouska, is this place, this country this—this world—is it magical?"

The woman gave her a surprised look.

"Magical? I wouldn't say that."

"Ma'cal, ma'cal," Bibby sang, bouncing on Ouska's hip.

"Well, you see," Cat tried to explain, "quite apart from the way I ended up here—in one big swoop, there was nothing I did that made it happen or anything I could have done to stop it—one minute I was looking at the bowl, and the next I was on my butt in the forest. But leaving that aside, I touched one of those trees in the forest, and it's like I got an electric shock or something..."

"Ah!" said Ouska. "Is that what that was?"

"What *what* was?"

"I felt that something happened, must have been right at that moment. I knew it had to do with Bibby, that's why I came looking for her. An Unissima sometimes feels other females more strongly than males, else I'd have known it had to do with the boy."

The boy? Oh, she meant Guy. Cat smiled to herself. "Boy"—he looked like he was close to thirty.

"But, don't you see, right there, that Unissima thing. You just know things, feel them in your bones or something? That sounds magical to me."

66

"Ah, well, that. I suppose you could call it magical if you will. We have our powers, of course. Don't you have them in your world?"

"Powers? No, I don't think so—unless you mean electricity or whatever."

"I don't know what that might be. No, I mean personal powers—the ability to make things work. A person's gift that works itself out in what they touch or what they can do. For us Unissimae, it's knowing things, generally things about people. I still think you are one yourself, although perhaps you have not come into your powers yet. Is your mother still alive?"

Cat gave her head a little shake. "My mother? Uh, honestly, I don't know. What's that got to do with anything?"

"How old would she be if she is living?"

"I'm not sure," Cat said, slightly confused. "I think she was quite young when I was born, eighteen or nineteen, so, somewhere in her forties? She took off when I was two and we never heard from her again; my grandparents raised me (my father was never in the picture in the first place). Why?"

"Your mother left when you were a babe?" Ouska gave Cat another sidelong, probing glance. "Just like this little one here." She gave Bibby a quick bounce on her hip, which made the little girl giggle. "I told you, an Unissima is an only daughter of an only daughter. She doesn't come into her powers until it's certain her mother won't have any other children. For me, it was when my mother died, I was twenty-two years old. The little one's mother was just fourteen when her mother went through the change—she

67

was a late-in-life babe (and spoiled rotten for it). She was just the right age to be foolish about the Knowing—too old to be accustomed to it from the start, as little Bibby will, and too young to have any sense of what that kind of gift means and how to use it properly."

"So what happened to her? You said she left? Or did she die? 'Cause otherwise, how would Bibby have her powers?"

"I don't know," Ouska said, "that's the thing. The woman disappeared one day, about a year ago, that's all we heard. The boy won't say what happened, won't speak of her at all. But he was left holding the babe, quite literally. And a few months after that, the little one showed signs of the Knowing, tiny though she was. And she couldn't have, not if her mother were still—but yet, my own Knowing tells me the woman's not dead."

A tabby cat scooted across the path in front of them, and Bibby squealed. "Gah!" she cried with a big smile, pointing at the animal.

"There!" said Cat. "I meant to ask you about that. That's what she calls me, Gah, and has done so right from the start. Does she know my name?"

"Seems that way, doesn't it? Having the Knowing doesn't mean she can pronounce things properly." Cat laughed, and Ouska gave a chuckle. "If your own mother is still alive and hasn't gone through the change yet, perhaps that's why you haven't got the Knowing yet. She didn't have any brothers or sisters from her mother, did she?"

"No," said Cat thoughtfully, "none that I know of. But—but I don't think in my world, we even *have* Unissimas, or whatever. People are just, you know, people. Some are really good at things, but most are just ordinary. Like me."

Ouska gave a snort. "You're not ordinary, girl, let me tell you. *She* knows that, don't you, pumpkin." She ruffled Bibby's feathery curls.

Cat looked down at her feet. She wasn't used to have someone read her like they were looking right into her soul, and even though Ouska was doing it in the kindest manner possible, it was still disconcerting. Her eyes fell on her bandaged hand.

"Ouska?" She turned her head and looked at the older woman's slightly snub-nosed profile. "You said that you have your powers. Do all of you have them? I mean, does everyone here have some kind of, I don't know, special ability? Like mind reading—well, okay, the Knowing—"

"Hold hard, girl, I can't read minds. And neither can Bibby here and never will, even though she's Unissima Maxima."

"Huh?"

"She's the only daughter of an Unissima, which makes her doubly strong in the Knowing. Nobody can do that, read minds. The Knowing—it's just, well, knowing things that others don't. As if someone had told you in your ear."

"Like intuition, you mean?"

"More than that. When you touched that tree, it sent a surge along that reached me almost immediately, and the Knowing said to me, 'There's something happened in the Wald, and it's to do with the little one.' I've learned to my cost not to ignore that voice, so I set out and found you all. Well, here we are."

"Here" turned out to be the first few houses of the village. Cat was rather surprised. They looked much more prosperous, and far less rustic, than Guy's cottage in the forest clearing. Half-timbering predominated, the neatly whitewashed brickwork between the dark-stained beams contrasting with the wood shingles on the roofs that had weathered to a soft grey. Flower boxes filled with bright blooms hung from the windowsills outside of small-paned windows, and wooden shutters stood ready to be closed against nightfall.

The forest track had become a hard-packed dirt road and then cobblestone paving, and now Ouska turned right and pushed down the iron door latch on a solid-looking, closely jointed wooden door. They stepped up into a kitchen, its floor laid with speckled brown ceramic tiles. A heavy deal table with benches on either side stood in the middle of room, a couple of chairs on the short ends, two Welsh dressers flanking the window that looked out over the side of the house. In the far wall was a fireplace, but unlike the open hearth in Guy's cottage, this was enclosed with black cast-iron doors, like a wood stove partially set into the wall. Above the fire was something that looked like a large, enamelled tank; to the left of the fireplace, a sink with a pump attached to it. Indoor running water! Things were looking up.

Ouska sat Bibby on one of the benches, from which the little girl promptly slid down.

"Kikigah!" she demanded.

"I don't know where the kittycat is," said Ouska. "Let's get her a saucer of milk, maybe she'll come." She took a shallow pottery dish from one of the dressers, glazed in the same brown as the dishes in the cottage. An unglazed pitcher, sitting in a dish of water and covered with a cheesecloth, proved to be a milk jug. Ah, thought Cat, the water acts as an evaporation cooler! Smart. Ouska put the dish on the ground, poured a little of the milk into it, and told Bibby to call the kitty.

"Kikiiii!"

"No, like this: *Pspspss*!" The older woman hissed out a sharp call. Immediately there came a soft thump from the room next to the kitchen, and around the open door a beautiful little calico cat padded into view.

"*Mrreow*?"

"Kiki!" squealed the baby, and pounced. The cat slid out of the way of the grasping little hands, padded over to the saucer, and settled down on her haunches to lap at her treat, apparently oblivious to the little girl who had caught up to her to happily pat her and pull her tail.

"Now, Catriona, you'll want a wash," said Ouska, opening a door next to the fireplace. Cat followed her through into a small room that backed onto the kitchen.

It was a bathroom! A full-fledged, real bathroom. The fixtures looked different from what Cat was used to, but they were easily recognizable as a washbasin and a tub, the latter a large wooden barrel with a spout coming through the wall directly from the big tank that was mounted above the fireplace in the kitchen. Running hot water! Cat hadn't expected this, it was fabulous.

Ouska walked out through another door and came back with a stack of linen.

"Here's a towel." She handed Cat a thick, white, woven sheet. "And you'll want to put that blouse and skirt back on after; mine are too wide and short for you. But you can have some of my underlinen, the drawers have a pullstring, and the shift is meant to be loose anyway." She put the garments on the edge of the washbasin, then turned the tap on the water pipe to send warm water gushing into the round wooden tub. "When you've finished, just pull out the stopper." She indicated something like a cork on the inside bottom edge of the tub. "It goes into a barrel out back. We use it to water the garden." Greywater collection—they even were environmentally friendly in this place. "And here's a piece of soap."

As soon as she closed the door behind her, Cat stepped out of her borrowed finery and climbed into the tub. It was just big enough for her to sit down with her knees drawn up under her chin and have the water come all the way up to her armpits. A hot sitz bath. Bliss.

Cat let her arms relax down into the water and gave a delicious shiver as the warmth gave her goosebumps all over. *Aaah.*

But wait! She had forgotten to take the bandage of her hand—in fact, she had forgotten about her hand being sore altogether. She'd just used it as if nothing had happened.

Puzzled, she unwound the cloth and wiggled her fingers. There was no sign of bruising, no evidence that a few hours earlier she had wondered if every bone in that hand had been cracked. Curious.

She slid down deeper into the warm water and let it soothe the kinks out of her body.

CHAPTER 10

WHEN CAT CAME BACK out of the bathroom half an hour later, trying to untangle her hair with her fingers, the kitchen smelled deliciously of something tangy and clean that got up into Cat's nose in a rather pleasant way.

"Where's Bibby?" Cat asked, looking around for the little girl.

"My Yldra took her off to play with her boy," Ouska said. "So we have a little time to ourselves. Would you like a cup of mintbrew?" She gestured at a round-bellied teapot sitting on the deal table.

"Mintbrew? Oh, you mean like tea? I'd love some!" That's what that lovely sinus-clearing smell was. "You wouldn't have a comb or something, would you? I can't seem to get my hair straight."

"Oh, yes, of course! And you've washed your hair with the soap, haven't you—you'll need a rinse for that, or it'll be like straw." Ouska reached into the bottom of the cupboard and brought out a stoppered bottle. "Here, that'll do, just use a bit of it."

"What is it?"

"Cider vinegar. You need something sour to smooth your hair again; soap's hard on it. Just take it to the bathroom. I'll get you that comb."

Catriona shrugged. She'd just had a bath in an oversized wooden bucket with water heated on a wood fire; she was wearing linen bloomers with a drawstring by way of underwear; she might as well be rinsing her hair with vinegar. When in Rome…

Except that she wasn't in Rome. She was in Isachang. Or rather, Samach. No, actually, Ruph. She felt quite proud of herself for remembering those names. It had always been one of her strengths at the library to retain little bits of information like that. Especially about people; customers really liked it when you addressed them by name after they had only been in once or twice.

However, she wasn't so sure how she'd do in this place; the names were so different, it was like learning a new language. A new challenge. Wasn't that what she had wanted when she quit her job? Well, she had it now, in spades. Cider vinegar for a hair rinse was the least of it. So, when in Ruph, do as the Ruphians do? Or were they called Ruffians?

Cat chuckled at her own joke as she hung her head over the wash basin in the bathroom, poured a little bit of vinegar into her hands and worked it into her hair. It stung in a small cut on her left index finger that she hadn't known she had. But when she had towelled off her hair again and used the comb Ouska had given her, she found that the wooden teeth slid smoothly and easily through her hair. She might smell like salad dressing now, but the vinegar worked as well as any conditioner she'd ever used!

"So, Catriona," Ouska said as they sat at the kitchen table, mugs of fragrant peppermint tea cupped in their hands, "you asked me something about the powers, earlier when we were walking."

Cat tried to remember. "Ah yes. You said everyone had powers, or you all had them, or something. *Do* you? I mean, does your husband, does—does Guy?"

"Uncle, certainly. He's the best brewman in the county. You had his applejack this morning, didn't you feel it?"

"You mean there was something magical about it? I thought it was just, you know, hard liquor."

"Oh, goodness, nothing magical. He just makes extremely good jack. And beer, and cider, and grape wine when he can get the fruit; really, he can make a fine drink out of anything he lays hands on. Mind you, I don't mean to say that there isn't something more to his drinks that those of other brewmen—more clout, for one, if he chooses—but then he's one of the Septimi. Of course they're all like that. Their oldest brother..."

"Septimi?"

"The Septimus family. We've got one of those in Ruph." She paused significantly, then took a look at Cat's puzzled face and gave a chuckle. "I keep forgetting you're not from here. Where you are from, are there people who lead, who are responsible for making sure things run right?"

"I suppose. We call them presidents or chairpersons or—"

"And what can they do, what is their special gift to put them in that position?"

Cat laughed.

"I don't know if there's anything special they can do, to be perfectly honest. Maybe convince others to vote for them, that's about it."

"Vote?" Ouska looked puzzled. "So there's no particular gift they have that makes them useful to the community?"

Cat shrugged, and Ouska shook her head.

"Peculiar," she said. "Well, here, where there is a Septimus family, they are the natural leaders of the town. They are the descendants of a seventh son, and they are specially gifted, with particular abilities to serve the people that no one else has to that extent. Not quite what in your words would be 'magic'—for the most part, it's just that extra gift within a gift that's rare to find in common folk. But with the Septimi, they all have it. And it's different in each of them. Never two in one generation that can do the same."

Cat took a sip from her mug.

"So your husband is one of that family, and he can make extra good, um, hard drinks?" Which, when you thought of it...

"That's it," Ouska said. Her eyes crinkled up at the corners. "Yes, I know. But making good food and drink for enjoyment *is* a way to serve the community."

She was doing it again! Cat was sure she hadn't spoken that thought out loud.

"It's not just liquor, either, that Uncle can make. You'll have to try his May bowl sometime. His brothers have other gifts," Ouska continued. "The eldest works with metals, iron for the most part; he built that stove and the water heater. Most ingenious thing, I wouldn't be without it now. The third brother, Eradlor, made the tub. Wood, metal, stone, music, colours, earth—growing food on the land—they each have their affinity."

"Do they all live in this town?" Cat asked. The place must be bigger than she'd thought.

"Not all—it's not as if they were obliged to stay. But some of them always do, and together, they keep the traditions and serve the people; they take it in turns to be head man when one is needed."

That sounded like a great system of community management.

Ouska nodded. She reached for the teapot and topped up their mugs.

"That's not all, though," she continued. "The Septimi are all gifted, but every once in so often, a really special one comes along. It's always the seventh son. There hadn't been one in generations, well over a hundred years, and then Salmor was born. He was Uncle's youngest brother."

Cat leaned forward on her elbows, fascinated, her forgotten tea rapidly cooling in her hands. "So what could he do?"

"As I said, he was the seventh Septimus of his generation. The seventh son's power is greater than those of the others, but above all different. He can guide people, and he usually has powers in his hands that others need tools for. I heard tell of one seventh son long ago who could make water boil in a cup just by holding it."

That could be inconvenient; Cat wondered if he burned himself doing that.

"Yes, well," Ouska said with a twitch at the corner of her mouth that likely meant she'd caught Cat's thought again. "It was a long time ago. The thing is that because that seventh Septimus has such a special gift, it's said that he can never be a craftsman like his brothers; he cannot use more than one gift." She made a "*hrumph*" noise in her throat and set her mug down on the table with enough force that a little of the tea slopped out.

"So, that seventh brother of your husband's—or, I suppose, sixth brother, seventh son altogether—Salmor?"

"Yes."

"So, Salmor. What was his gift, and what became of him?"

"Well, he was the Septimus—*the* Septimus. He decided to expand the village and have new wells dug towards the outskirts, and it was his idea to bring the water from those wells to all the houses." She pointed at the pump by the sink. "His brothers helped with the particulars, of course, but it was his hands that put the pieces together, and that's what made it all work."

She took a thoughtful sip from her cup.

"He was a good man, was Salmor. It's nearly three years now he's been gone."

"Oh, I'm sorry," said Cat.

They were silent for a moment.

"So then," Cat began again, "who takes care of the village now? Salmor's brothers? Or does it pass to his children—if he had any?"

"Didn't I say?" Ouska got up and put the teapot back on the dresser. "Of course he had children," she said over her shoulder. "He was Guy's father."

CHAPTER 11

"Guy's father?" Cat should have seen it coming. "Guy is one of that Septimus family? Then, that's why—"

Ouska turned her head, rather quickly.

"Why what?"

Cat held out her right hand, without bandage and completely whole.

"He touched it again, just before you came back this morning. I don't know what he did, but, look." She flexed her fingers, made a fist, then flattened it out again.

There was a curious gleam in Ouska's eyes, but she shook her head.

"I've never heard of a Septimus being able to do that. They're craftsmen. Guy is—"

There was a knock, immediately followed by the appearance of a head around the edge of the door.

"Mother?" A young woman stepped into the room, her red-blonde hair wreathed around her head in the same coronet style Ouska wore. She was carrying Bibby, and a white-blond little boy trailed into the kitchen after her.

"Mother, the goat is having trouble with the kids," she said, putting Bibby down. "Can you come help? I'm sorry, I can't look after both the little ones and the goat at the same time..."

She caught sight of Cat, whose chair was partially hidden behind the open door.

"Oh, I didn't see you there!" She smiled at Cat. "You must be the visitor? I'm Yldra, and this is my Randy." The little boy critically assessed Cat from behind his mother's skirts. "I'm sorry to be rushing in here like this, but, Mother," she turned back to Ouska, her voice taking on urgency, "I'm really worried about that goat."

The older woman was already opening cupboards and drawers and taking out a collection of supplies, presumably for the midwifery of bothersome goats. She looked at Cat.

"I was going to keep you here for a while, Catriona, you and the babe, but now it looks like I'm needed. In fact, we might have need of Uncle as well. Think you can find your way back to the cottage? It would be a big help if you could send him out to us; just tell him his daughter's goat is having trouble with the kidding."

Cat smiled wryly. The people in this place seemed rather crisis-prone.

"All right," she said. "Is there anything I can do here still to help? Lock up, turn things down..."

"No, we've got it. If you can just take the little one with you, we'll all be off." Ouska's matter-of-fact tone said she had no doubt that Cat could handle anything that was coming her way. Cat pulled back her shoulders. She would not disappoint her.

"Come on, munchkin!" She scooped up the little girl and settled her on her hip like she had seen Ouska do. "Let's go see your papa."

"Yee bubba?"

"Yes, go see Papa."

"Bibby Gah yee Bubba!"

"That's right, you and me go see." Cat smiled down at the baby and tapped her on her freckled nose with the tip of her finger, which made the little girl giggle.

Cat looked up to see Ouska's brown eyes on her. There was that gleam again.

Twenty minutes later, they were back at the cottage and delivered the message to Uncle, who muttered something under his breath about being the village nursemaid and promptly set out for his daughter's house. Cat was pretty sure that he was actually rather proud that nobody seemed to be able to do without him.

As the door closed behind the burly man, Cat turned to look around the cottage. Guy was propped up in his bed, eating some soup out of one of those brown pottery bowls. He looked a vast deal better than when Cat had seen him last, much cleaner, for one. He was wearing a white linen shirt, laced up at the throat, and his bed was now properly made up with clean sheets and a nice, soft grey blanket with a woven-in blue stripe down the side (Cat looked around for the ratty brown blanket that Ouska had been so disgusted with, and found it bundled in the corner by the fireplace).

Guy's hair, now that it was not smeared with clay, turned out to be a darker shade of red than that of his cousin Yldra; it was long enough to brush his collar, and by the way it sprang back from his forehead and waved around his face it was easy to tell from whom his little girl had inherited her feathery red curls. Even though he was still pale, his face had lost that horrible grey hue, and his eyes were much clearer than they had been.

Cat made up her mind to stop being embarrassed about being in the cottage with him. After all, if she were a nurse, this would be perfectly normal, right? So she'd simply consider herself a nurse. Not that she had any medical knowledge... Or a babysitter, that was a role she was more familiar with. Except that when she was babysitting, back in her teens, she was never stuck in a rustic cottage with the sick father of the baby she was looking after. Oh dear...

She cast a sidelong glance at Guy's face and saw that he was looking at her just as awkwardly. Their eyes met, and they both gave a nervous chuckle. Bibby looked from one of them to the other and let out a high-pitched giggle, which sounded so funny that both Cat and Guy had to laugh in earnest. After that, there was no more room for tension or awkwardness.

Cat smiled at Guy. "Good soup?"

He smiled back, an attractive lopsided grin that crinkled up the corner of his eye.

"The best, Aunt made it. I'm to eat every last drop. There's more in the pot on the table, if you want some—Cat?"

"Gah," confirmed Bibby, then tried out the combination of their names. "Bubbagah. Bubbagah youp."

"Yes, that's right!" said Cat. The little girl was really not hard to understand once you got used to her way of talking. "Papa and Cat are eating soup. And Bibby too." She sat the baby on the bench by the table and brought over two more pottery bowls.

Suddenly she felt Guy's eyes on her, watching her handling of the dishes.

"Your hand?" he asked, his voice quiet.

Wordlessly, she held it out, turned it palm upwards, and wiggled her fingers. A look of relief crossed his face, followed by something that felt as if shutters were being closed. Cat wondered what was going on with him, but this was hardly the time to ask.

By the time Cat and Bibby had finished their soup—a thick vegetable stew with lentils and some tasty seasonings Cat couldn't quite identify—the little girl was yawning.

"Looks like someone needs a nap!" Cat said.

"Yes, and Bibby looks sleepy, too," replied Guy from the bed. He surprised a laugh out of Cat, but a glance at his face showed that he looked grey around the edges again, and he drooped against the pillow.

"Very well," Cat said in her best imitation of Ouska's no-nonsense voice, "a nap it is. But Bibby goes potty first."

She took the little girl by the hand, led her out the front door, and turned left around the adjacent building. The water pump was on the corner of the building, and next to it Cat noticed an entrance into the annex, with a large window beside it. Some twenty yards away from the back corner of the building was a strange beehive-shaped structure built of piled-up bricks, about four or five feet high and as much across, with a round curved tunnel leading into it from one side. No, not a beehive, thought Cat, an igloo! A tall, straight-sided brick igloo, with a rather small entrance. Curious.

They turned the corner again, walked along the back wall of the annex, and went around the next corner to the privy. It seemed a bit of a long trek around the building to get to the outhouse, when it was stuck right to the back wall of the house, Cat thought; then she noticed a door in the annex wall at a right angle to the privy door. She tried the latch, but it was locked from the inside.

When they returned to the cottage, Guy looked like he was ready to drop off to sleep.

"You know, you can go through the workshop to get out back," he said, his voice rough with the sudden fatigue of illness.

"Oh, I see. No Bibby, your bed is over here!" Cat said, as the little girl attempted to climb up on the bed. She reached out to scoop the baby up, but Guy weakly shook his head, with a light contraction of his eyebrows.

"She always sleeps with me," he said. With an obvious effort, he reached out his arm and pulled the little girl closer to his side; she snuggled against him and gave a deep, satisfied sigh. Guy pulled the blanket over both of them and closed his eyes in exhaustion.

In just a few minutes, their regular breathing showed that they had both fallen asleep.

CHAPTER 12

C AT WASN'T SURE WHAT to do next. The dishes needed washing, but how did one heat water in this place? Probably over the fire in some way, but she had no idea how. Besides, the clatter would wake up the sleepers on the bed. So the dishes would have to wait. And there wasn't really anything else to do...

Her eyes fell on the door beside the fireplace. The workshop! She might as well do some exploring; if nothing else, she could look for the shorter route to the privy out back.

The door was a plank door and, like the front door, opened inwardly. In fact, it looked like it had begun life as another exterior door; the annex must be a later addition to the cottage.

Cat found herself stepping down off the doorstep into a room almost one and a half times as big as the cottage. It was lit by the window that looked out on the brick beehive-igloo, next to the outside door Cat had seen on her way to the privy. In the middle of the room stood a solid-looking table, its top covered with tightly stretched canvas stained a reddish brown. Along the wall to Cat's left ran long floor-to-ceiling shelves, half full of unglazed terracotta pots. The arts-and-crafts smell of clay was in her nostrils again, and finally the realization clicked into place: of course, Guy was a potter!

Suddenly things made sense. He had been digging clay from the pit in the forest when he injured himself. The brown pottery dishes in his and Ouska's house were his own work. And the beehive thing—the beehive was the kiln! Cat was quite proud of herself for recognizing it. She'd seen pictures in reference books back at the library.

Pottery: Dewey decimal 738. Cat had to make an effort to come up with the call number. Thoughts of the library seemed very remote. Was it really less than twenty-four hours since she had been plucked out of her placid ex-librarian's existence in Greenward Falls and been hurled into this new world—this new, ancient world? A world where a matter-of-fact woman read Cat's mind, told her she was a capable person and not ordinary, expected her as a matter of course to care for an injured man and a small girl who had the strange gift of Knowing; where a man asked her to marry him in the night, crushed her hand in the morning and cured it again an hour later; where a little girl with feathery red curls called Cat by her name, fell asleep in her arms, and planted herself firmly in Cat's heart... Really just twenty-four hours?

Cat turned around. To the left of the door into the cottage stood a tall cupboard, rather like a wardrobe, its doors firmly closed. In the corner between it and the shelves full of unglazed pottery was another plank door, the bolt that latched it shot into place.

She pulled back the bolt, opened the door, and stuck her head outside. Aha! Mission accomplished: there was the privy, in the corner formed by the house and the workshop that jutted just a bit further into the garden. So now she knew the interior way to the outhouse.

Next to the privy, attached to the back of the cottage, was a low, sloping roof covering a neatly stacked pile of firewood, and a jumble of assorted equipment. Cat thought she could make out a hoe and a shovel; probably gardening tools. Beyond the wood pile a wattle fence stuck out some ten or twelve feet into the forest, a gate made of woven sticks in the middle. That would be the garden then.

Cat stepped back into the workshop, latching the door behind her. Beside the door that led into the cottage was a fireplace, smaller than the one on the other side of the wall but obviously sharing its chimney, and next to that a contraption that it took Cat a few moments to identify: the potter's wheel! Of course, that would be a potter's chief tool.

It was set into a wooden frame, about three feet high and four feet long and wide. On one side was mounted a bench, on the other a shelf held a jar with various wire loop tools and pointy things sticking out of it, a bowl with pieces of sponge and a strip of something that looked like leather, and a bucket of muddy water. In the middle of the whole thing was the wheel itself. Its top was a metal disk, about a foot across, with concentric grooves cut into it. It was attached by a two-foot-high straight shaft to another disk at the bottom. Cat thought that one might be called the flywheel. It looked for all the world like it was carved out of a solid hunk of granite, two-and-a-half feet across and something like six inches thick. It had to be phenomenally heavy.

Cat reached out a hand and experimentally pushed the wheel with her finger. It didn't even budge. She grasped the edge of the top disk and tried to make it spin; when it still didn't move, she grabbed it with both hands like a steering wheel and tried to turn it—gently at first, then finally she twisted as hard as she could. Lazily the wheel spun into motion, slowly turning around, and around, and around, and around...

I wonder how long it'll keep doing that, Cat thought. The smooth, silent motion was starting to make her dizzy, so she turned away. There was lots more to explore in the room.

On the remaining wall of the room, running around the corner to the outside door, more shelving was mounted, most of it open slat work that held partially finished pieces. There were rows of cups without handles, their bottoms jagged and uneven, and on the shelf below them a board with lids that didn't have any knobs on them. The edges of those pieces were a much paler red than the rest, as if they were drying from the outside in. Cat wondered if they were supposed to do that, or if Guy had meant to get back to them as soon as he came back with the clay from the pit.

There were nondescript shapes concealed under pieces of oilcloth, probably meant to be protected from the fate of the prematurely drying cups and lids, while on one of the top shelves stood four lovely finished round-bellied teapots, lids and all, drying slowly as the air circulated around them. On the shelf below that were stacks of already-dry plates, in sizes that were anywhere from saucer to dinner plate. The bowls stacked on the next shelf down confirmed Cat's conclusion: they were the very shape of the soup bowls in the cottage and at Ouska's house, so definitely Guy's work.

The wheel kept spinning behind Cat, leisurely circling around, and around, ever more slowly. She looked past it to the big cupboard. What was in there that warranted having its doors so tightly closed? It was a tall piece of furniture, some seven feet high and about five feet wide, made from some kind of light wood, now mellowed to a greyish shade. The doors had shallow designs carved into them, swooping S-curves that met in the middle; the round doorknobs and the edges of the doors were liberally decorated with red-brown clay stains, the right-hand knob clearly showing the print of a thumb and three fingers.

Cat gave an experimental pull on the clay-printed doorknob, and to her surprise, with a soft creak the cupboard door swung open. More dishes—finished ones, here. The front of the cupboard at Cat's eye level was full of glazed ware, cups and bowls and plates and platters and serving dishes in various shades of brown, some plain, others with interesting dribble effects in the glaze. But a little lower down, Cat saw a pot in a pretty mossy green, and next to it and a little behind, a number of cups with a blueish sheen.

Carefully she took out one of them. There was a curious pierced-hole pattern running all over it, in a quite regular, geometric way, like perforations. Nice—but why holes, in a mug? She reached for another one. Also holes, but these ones randomly scattered all over the surface of the dish. And another, and another. Maybe they were meant for wind lights? But then, there, that was a brown milk jug like the one in the cottage, and it had holes in just three places, right below the pour spout. And here was a green mug that had holes right in the bottom. What was the point of that? They were beautiful pots, but those holes were weird.

And all the dishes with the holes were on the lowest shelves. A thin layer of dust covered them, as if they had been tucked out of sight some time ago and not been handled since. On the very lowest shelf, at the bottom of the cupboard, were some quite attractive cups in the moss-green glaze. Were they full of holes too? Cat squatted down to see. She pulled one out and wiped the dust off; the pot felt cool and pleasant in her hand, and there were no holes in it that Cat could see. Why was it left to gather dust on the bottom shelf?

Behind the cups Cat spotted a fat shape. She thought it looked like one of the round-bellied teapots, like the one Ouska had that Cat liked a lot, except this one was green. She reached in, found a handle to take hold of, and carefully pulled the pot out.

Something came with it, making a soft metallic clinking noise against the ceramic. A short, tarnished silver chain, black with age and tangled around itself, was caught on a small decorative protrusion on the spout of the teapot.

Cat put the teapot on the plank floor and cautiously worked the chain loose from the spout. When it came free, Cat saw that it was not only tarnished, but in several places it was bent, as if someone had tried to tear or crush the fine-linked piece. In the middle of the chain, barely attached by a half-open ring, hung a broken pendant.

It had been a bird, a delicate little swallow in flight. The black tarnish nearly obscured the fine detail of the filigree, but Cat could make out the bird's head, could see how its tiny beak had been open in cheerful song as it flew. The ring was attached to its back, between the spread wings, but now all that was left was one wing of the bird and its head.

Someone had savagely snapped the delicate pendant in half.

CHAPTER 13

THE MORNING SUNLIGHT FLOODED Ouska's kitchen, where Cat and Bibby sat at the table eating thick porridge laced with honey, fragrant mint tea steaming in Cat's mug.

"I sure slept well last night," Cat said to Ouska, who was stirring the porridge on the lip of the wood stove that jutted out from the fireplace. "Your spare bed is a lot more comfortable than Guy's rocking chair, especially when you have to share sleeping quarters with little people." She smiled at the baby, who sported a beautiful milk moustache.

"Bibby leep!" announced the little girl.

"Yes, you were asleep too."

"Bibby wake!"

"And then you woke up," agreed Cat.

"Bibby pay now!"

"You want to do what?"

"Pay. Pay kiki."

"Oh, play with the kitty. I don't know where the kitty is; why don't you go see if you can find her?" Cat took the tea towel that the little girl wore by way of a bib and wiped the milk and smeared porridge off her face with it, and she slid off the bench and toddled off to find the cat.

"I hope the men did all right in the cottage last night," Cat said.

Ouska chuckled. "Oh yes, I expect so. Provided the boy could sleep through Uncle's snoring. That man can rattle the windows when he's in top form. But I was glad to see the wound getting so much better; won't be long before that young fool will be champing at the bit to get back to his work."

Cat smiled. She had the feeling that Ouska's "fool" meant precisely nothing when it came to her nephew.

"He sure makes nice dishes," she said, admiring the mug in her hand. "They feel just right. Those are all his work, aren't—"

A yowl and a shriek from the next room interrupted her. Cat jumped to her feet, but Ouska was already at the door of the parlour where a wailing Bibby stumbled out, holding out her pudgy little hand with a thin red scratch line across it.

"Kiki bad! Bibby owie!" she sobbed.

Ouska scooped her up in a comforting hug.

"Tush, tush," she soothed, then she looked over Bibby's head at Cat. "Well, had to happen sooner or later. Hopefully it'll teach her some respect for the cat." She bore the baby off to the bathroom to clean the scratch. The small cat nonchalantly padded into the kitchen, sat on the hearthrug, stuck her back leg into the air, and proceeded to lick her bottom.

"And that, I suppose," said Cat, "is what you think of all that, is it?"

A knock sounded on the outside door. When Cat opened it, she found a quite pretty girl of about fifteen standing outside. She had long, glossy dark hair, and even though her blouse and skirt didn't seem to be cut much differently from what Cat herself was wearing at the moment, she had managed to tuck and lace them in so cleverly that it showed off every curve of her figure. On her arm hung a cloth-covered basket.

"Can I help you?"

"Oh! Oh, I was looking for the wisewoman! I got eggs for her," the girl held out the basket, "and my mother wants more of the balm leaves for the face cream, she's running low."

"Why don't you come in then; the—the wisewoman should be right out," Cat said, turning back into the kitchen.

The girl stepped up over the door sill and gave Cat a nosy look.

"Your skirt and blouse, they look just like Ashya's!" she said.

Rather a curious introduction.

"They were loaned to me. Who is Ashya? I'm new here, I don't know people yet."

"You don't know about Ashya? I thought you were one of *her* family." She tipped her head in the direction of the back parts of the house, indicating Ouska.

"No. I met her nephew, and her husband, and—I suppose Bibby is a great-niece."

"Ooh, the little darling!" cooed the girl. She put on a sugary smile, then immediately dropped it again. "But if you know Bibby, you must know who Ashya—who she *was*." She leaned forward conspiratorially and lowered her voice to a near whisper. "You know what I think? I think *he* killed her!"

"Uh—pardon me?"

"You know, *him*! The *potter*." She pronounced the word with a sneer. "He's got a *filthy* temper, Ashya told me so herself. We're cousins, you know." She flounced around and settled herself on the bench by the table. "Ashya, she said he was such an *awfully* jealous husband, *and* mean, wouldn't let her out of his *sight* or do *anything* she wanted *or* get her anything *nice*. And then she had the baby,"—another flounce—"and he got *totally* unreasonable, wouldn't even let her leave that *filthy* little shack out in the Wald, and expected her to be nothing but a *drudge* for that kid. And if she tried to get her own way just a *teensy* bit, he'd fly off into a jealous *rage*! She told me so *herself*. And then,"—there was that dramatic whisper again—"she *disappeared*!"

"Mm-hmm." Cat nodded her head in her best listening manner, an art she had perfected at the library through countless rants by patrons insistent on sharing the latest conspiracy theories with her. Nod and make agreeing noises, while letting the sound go in one ear and out the other.

"Well, it's *true*! Nobody's seen her since that day last summer—not this past one, the one before—when she came into town, just to do a *teensy* bit of shopping, they say, and then *he* came after her, all smeared with his filthy clay, and dragged her home by the *hair*, they say. *And*,"—she opened her eyes wide in a dramatic gesture, obviously relishing every detail of her recital—"somebody heard *screaming* from that house, and ... *nobody's—seen—her—since.*"

"Uh-huh," said Cat noncommittally.

"Yes! Ooh, and you know, the same thing happened to *him*!"

Now Cat was thoroughly confused.

"Guy disappeared too?"

"No, no, not him, *his brother*! You know," the girl leaned forward again, every inch the conspirator, "the *Septimissimus*! *Everyone* knows he's filthy jealous of him, because he was only the sixth, and *Sepp*, he's seventh, so *he* had all the *gift,* and they were *always* fighting, from the time they were small—and then Sepp, he had a *screaming* fight with him in the street last week, they say, and the next day he went to his house, in the woods, and *he* disappeared too! I wonder what happened." Another flounce. "Sepp's really *cute*. I'm going to marry him, you know." She flipped her dark hair back over her shoulder.

"If Sepp's disappeared, that would be a little difficult, wouldn't it?" That had just slipped out. This girl was getting on Cat's nerves.

The girl drew a breath. "Well..." she began.

"Kashinka!" Ouska's voice was sharp as she stepped back in the room.

The girl leaped off the bench, all signs of the conspiracy theorist gone.

"Oh, oh, w-wisewoman!" she stammered. "Here's e-eggs, and mother wants more balm leaves for the face cream!"

"Very well," Ouska said briefly. She looked out the required leaves and made short shrift of sending the girl on her way.

Cat looked at Ouska in surprise. The older woman banged the empty porridge bowls from the table into a stack and set them on the dresser with a thump; with a loud clatter she took the lid off the water kettle and gave the pump handle a few vicious yanks.

"Fool!" she finally said. "Utter fool, that Kashinka! Conceited, empty-heading, silly, self-absorbed, nasty little gossiping *fool*!" There was an entirely different tone to that "fool" now. "But they're all like that, the whole family." She slammed the kettle on the top of the fireplace cook surface.

"Is it true she's Guy's wife's cousin?"

"Yes, unfortunately. And that was about the only true thing she told you."

"You heard what she said then?"

"The last bit. The rest I already heard before, often enough. It's nonsense, tomfoolery—most of it, at any rate. Don't believe a word of it!" she said fiercely.

"Most of it? Then some of it is true? What about this Septimississi..." Cat stumbled over the syllables.

"Septimissimus? Yes, that's true enough. Well, that the seventh son of the seventh Septimus—you'll recall what I told you—that he's double strong in the Powers. We call him the Septimissimus. Yes, we have one right now; that only happens once every few hundred years, if that."

"Guy's brother?"

"He's got a younger brother, yes. Sepp. Young fool," she added, but it came out like she said it unthinkingly, and once again her fond tone of voice gave the lie to the insult. "He's not much more than a year younger than the boy, turned twenty-eight Thursday last. That Kashinka's nonsense about them fighting in the street—sometimes I'd like to take a paddle to that girl. Of course the boys fought when they were small; they're brothers, aren't they? They're fond enough of each other, and they've long outgrown the fisticuffs."

"So where is he now, that Sepp?"

Ouska looked thoughtful.

"That I can't tell you. The worst of that silly girl's lies is that there's the odd half-truth hid in them, like a needle stuck in a piece of cloth that jabs you when you least expect it. Sepp—well, the boy always had a hankering to fly the coop, to see the world. He's not like his brother. Guy belongs here, he's rooted in the earth he works with, but Sepp—no. For the last while, some months now, he has been more and more out of sorts, and a week ago it got rather so even people who didn't know him well noticed. He might have snapped at his brother when they met in the street that day, but by then he was snapping at everyone. And it's true enough that the last time anyone saw him he was headed down the path to the pottery."

"So Guy was the last person to see him? What does he say about it?"

The older woman gave a brief grunt.

"Nothing—what do you expect?"

She leaned over the table to wipe the porridge splatters from Bibby's spot, and a silver pendant on a necklace, slightly darkened with tarnish, swung free from the neckline of her blouse.

"That's a nice necklace," Cat said. "I never noticed it before! Do you always wear it?"

Ouska reached for the necklace, pulled it outwards from her neck, and screwed her eyes downwards to look at the pendant.

"Oh dear, that's black! Needs cleaning." She reached behind her head, unclasped the necklace, and took it off. "Yes, it's my wedding chain. That's not been off my neck for more than a few minutes in the last forty years."

Cat picked up the necklace from the table where Ouska had put in down. The pendant was shaped like a small animal—a circular centre, with five little stubs protruding from it, one of which formed the loop that suspended it from the chain. A turtle, Cat though, looking like it was hanging onto the chain with its teeth.

"Wedding chain?"

"Yes, it's the sign of the marriage, the contract, if you will. Uncle gave it to me for our wedding." Ouska placed a grey metal dish, like a small pie plate, on the table. "Pass me the salt cellar, will you?" When Cat gave her the ceramic pot, she held out her hand for the necklace. Intrigued, Cat watched as the older woman put the necklace in the bottom of the dish and sprinkled a teaspoon of salt over it.

"Is it always an animal on the pendant?" she asked.

"Most often. But sometimes it's a tree, or a flower. Always a living thing, though; it says that as long as the chain is whole, the marriage will live." Ouska fetched the kettle from the stove top. "That's what I meant when I said it's the contract—you can break the marriage if you wilfully break the necklace."

She poured boiling water from the kettle onto the salt-covered necklace in the dish. A sharp, metallic smell rose with the steam, and when it cleared, Cat saw that the chain and pendant in the water were bright silver again. Low-tech silver immersion polish—how clever!

Ouska fished the necklace out the water with a fork, rinsed it under the pump, then dried it with a soft cloth and clasped it around her neck again. She tucked the brightly gleaming pendant under her blouse.

"Better check on the babe," she said. "I left her playing with a doll on my bed; it's so quiet she's either gone to sleep or got up to mischief."

CHAPTER 14

OUSKA WAS ABSOLUTELY RIGHT about Guy. When Cat returned to the cottage (without Bibby, who was playing with her cousins in the village for a few hours), the potter and his uncle were in the middle of an argument about whether it was prudent for Guy to get back to his work already.

"I need to get things done!" he insisted. "I told you, I feel fine. But I'm going crazy just sitting here with you." He limped through the door into his workshop.

Uncle shook his head.

"Champing at the bit, the young fool," he muttered through his thick, greying beard.

Cat chuckled.

"That's just what your wife said he'd be doing," she told him, "in exactly those words."

The corner of his mouth twitched up in a lop-sided, eye-crinkling grin that was the mirror image of his nephew's.

"Well, the Woman, she knows," he said. "If she thinks that's what would happen, and she hasn't sent any messages that I should keep the boy tied to his bed, then that's good enough for me." He stood up. "Fact is, I need to get back to my own work; I've got a cider needs racking today. Should have happened yesterday, but, well, needs must." He nodded his head in the direction of the workshop. "One extra day won't have harmed my brew, but I don't want to leave it longer than absolutely necessary. Think you can manage here with him?"

Cat was feeling shy again.

"I think so…" She felt a blush climbing her face and was so embarrassed by it she blushed even more.

"You'll do, girl," said Uncle, patting her on the shoulder as he crossed the room to pick up his leather satchel from the floor in the corner.

Cat drew in a breath. Why did she feel as if she had just received a seal of approval? He likely didn't mean anything more than that she'd be okay for the rest of the afternoon—or did he?

Uncle slung his satchel over his shoulder so the strap ran across his deep barrel chest.

"There's some of the soup and bread left to eat, and more ointment and bandages are in the box on the shelf," he said. "I patched him up just a little while ago; the wound is coming along nicely. He'll have to be careful with it, but that's not something you can force on him. I'll be off then." He gave Cat a nod of his head that was almost a small bow, and with that he walked out the door.

Cat wasn't sure what to do with herself now. She looked around the cottage. All was clean and tidy. The dishes had been washed and the beds straightened, both Guy's platform bed under the window and the large pallet in the corner that Uncle had slept on. A small fire gently crackled to itself in the fireplace, spreading a pleasant warmth through the room.

She wondered if there was a fire in the hearth on the workshop side, too, and figured she might as well investigate.

Guy stood in the corner of the room by the drying shelves, examining the cups and lids that Cat had looked at the previous day. He had put on a clay-smeared washleather apron that covered him to the knees and rolled up his tunic sleeves to the elbows, and he wore a pair of clay-splattered half boots. When he heard the shop door creak he looked up and raised his eyebrows in greeting.

"These are ruined, I think," he said, gesturing at Cat with one of the lids. "Too dry now to put the knob on. Ah well, we start again." He chucked the lid into a bucket that sat on the floor between the wheel and the shelf, half full of dried-up pottery pieces.

The lid hit with a dull *thwack* and broke.

Cat gasped. Did he discard his work so casually?

Guy looked up at the sound and gave her his crooked smile.

"There's plenty more where that came from," he said, sending half a dozen mugs without handles after the lid. "It's not a waste, I'll reuse it. As long as it's not fired, the clay can be re-softened and made into new things, over and over if need be."

"Couldn't you salvage these? Seems a shame to throw them out!"

"No, the handles won't stick now; they'd just crack off during drying—or worse, in the firing, and then it really would be a waste. A fired crackpot is no use whatever. And believe me, these are no great loss, I can easily make more." He weighed another cup in his hand. "And besides," he said, his eyes narrowing, "sometimes it just feels good to do *this*." With the last word he hurled the cup into the bucket with such violence that it shattered into a hundred pieces, half of the shards bouncing back out.

He made a huffing noise, halfway between a scoff and a laugh, then he caught sight of Cat's face.

"Sorry," he said, his lopsided grin flashing out, "didn't mean to scare you." He dropped the remaining dried-up pieces into the bucket much more gently, crushing them down with his fist to make them fit.

"We'll slake them down later," he said. "All right, that's that. On to new work."

He limped over a few paces, then awkwardly squatted down on the ground, stretching his injured leg out straight to the side to keep from having to bend it. He stuck his fingers into what Cat had taken for a knot hole in the plank flooring and pulled upwards. A section of the floor came up, showing itself to be a trap door covering a large hollow space beneath. Guy balanced himself on the edge of the opening with one hand, reached into the cavity with the other, and lifted out an oilcloth-wrapped bundle about the size of Cat's head.

Cat peered into the hole; it was full of these bundles and smelled strongly of clay. Guy put the lump beside the opening, closed the trap door, and tried to lift the bundle and stand up at the same time, but he nearly lost his balance.

"Ouch!" With a thud, the bundle dropped to the floor again as he caught himself on the edge of the table and pulled to a full standing position.

"Here, I got it!" Cat sprang forward to keep him from bending again, grabbed the lump in both hands—and her eyes nearly started from their sockets. She could barely lift the thing! It had to be at least twenty, if not thirty, pounds.

With a grunt she heaved it onto the table. "Oof, that's no small peas!"

Guy chuckled. "Thanks," he said, pulling the oilcloth from the bundle and revealing a lump of reddish-brown clay. He looked around, then turned and tried to take a step. He winced as he put weight on his bad leg.

"Could you...?"

"What do you need?"

"The cutting wire. With the other tools." He pointed at the jar on the shelf of the wheel.

"Cutting wire? Oh, is this it?" From between the loopy tools and shaping sticks in the jar, Cat retrieved a twenty-inch length of thin wire, its ends tied around short pieces of dowelling.

"Yes, exactly. Thank you."

Guy balanced himself on his good leg. He grasped the wire by its dowel handles, snapped it tight between his hands, then garrotted the lump of clay in half. He picked up the upper half, gave it a quarter turn, then slammed it back down on the lower half with such force that Cat could feel it clear through the floorboards. He lifted the lump, brought it down on the wire, sliced, turned, slammed, over and over.

"What are you doing that for?" Cat asked curiously.

"Gets the air bubbles out." He gave the lump a final smack, then began wiring it into smaller pieces.

He put most of them to one side, then took one that was still a good eight inches in diameter and began kneading it on the canvas surface of the table. Both hands cupped the clay, squeezed inward, rolled thumbs-upward towards his body, released, squeezed again, and rolled. It was a swift motion, almost hypnotic in its steady rhythm. After a few minutes, the piece of clay was turned into a squat cylinder, rather like a ram's head, with a stub nose and two horns spiralling on the sides where he had grasped it and rolled it towards himself. Guy picked the piece up, slapped one of the ram's horns into his left palm, and smacked it into a rounded mound, continuing to rotate it in his palm in the same direction as the rolled ram's head. He placed it to the side, then picked up the next lump and began to knead it the same way.

Cat watched, fascinated.

"What does that do?" she asked.

"Makes it ready for throwing."

"Throwing?" Cat was having visions of pieces of clay being chucked against the wall. The strange things potters did... She wondered why, and unconsciously mimed the idea, moving her hand as if she was tossing a beanbag.

Guy laughed.

"No, not that kind of throwing. Turning it on the wheel, shaping it—it's called wheel-throwing."

"Oh." Cat felt a bit sheepish, but then, how was she supposed to have known? "Can I try this kneading thing?"

"Wedging," he corrected. "Sure, go ahead."

Cat picked up one of the smaller lumps—even that probably weighed two or three pounds!—and tried to squeeze her hands around it the way she saw him doing. All she succeeded in was squishing a hole into the clay with her thumbs, and it refused to be rocked towards her.

"Uh..."

"Never handled clay before? You'd better start smaller."

He wired a small chunk off the lump, perhaps a third the size of the whole, and held it out to her.

"Put your hands on either side, like so." He demonstrated with the remaining piece. "Then squeeze, and turn."

"Oh, sort of the way you'd hold your hand to unscrew a pickle jar lid, except on both sides at once and with the jar lying on its side," she said, delighted that she understood.

"Eh?"

"Um, never mind. I guess you don't have screw-top jars here."

Cat's little piece of clay nicely fitted inside her hand, and after a few attempts she was able to squeeze and roll it.

"Look, it's making that ram's face!" she said proudly.

"I've always called it a bull's head," he said, "but yes, it is. Well done."

Cat looked up to see that in the time she had half kneaded—no, wedged—her little piece, he had finished three more.

"Do you want this one too?" she asked.

Guy shook his head. "These will do me for now."

Ah, of course. He could also have said, "No, your amateurish effort is useless for me, you've spoiled that piece of clay," which Cat was sure would be nothing but the truth, but he didn't. That was nice of him.

He scooped up the wedged pieces two to a hand, then limped over to the pottery wheel and deposited them on the shelf. With a frown he looked into the water bucket.

"Hmm. I suppose that's enough to go on with," he said.

Awkwardly, he manoeuvred his injured leg past the shaft of the wheel and sat down on the bench seat of the wheel frame. He rested his left leg, slightly stretched out to favour the wound, on the sidebar of the frame, and propped his other foot on a corresponding bar on the right, while he fished with his hand in the water bucket. He brought out a small sponge, squeezed out most of the water, and wiped down the wheel head.

Cat had stopped wrestling with her chunk of clay and turned to watch him.

He picked up the first of the rounded clay mounds, then smacked it down hard on the wheelhead, dead centre. His right foot came off the sidebar, and then kicked the flywheel, hard, rhythmic kicks, faster and faster.

The wheel spun into motion, hummed, flew. His hand reached out, he squeezed the sponge in the water bucket, brought it out dripping, and discharged it over the whirling clay mound. Muddy water flew off the wheel, splattering the wall, the side of the fireplace, his apron (*Ah*, thought Cat, *that's what that's for!*).

Then he braced his elbows against his hips and cupped the clay on the wheel between his hands. He pushed it together so it spun perfectly centred, then squeezed up.

It rose into a column with a dome on top.

"It's a hoodoo!" Cat said.

"What?" Guy looked up, his hands playing the spinning clay.

"Oh, it's just that where I come from we have these stone or earth columns in some places, they look just like what you're making there. They're called hoodoos."

"Ah, I've heard of something like that, out on the Plains."

"Exactly, on the Prairies."

He turned his attention back to the wheel. The hoodoo under his hands changed, growing taller and thinner; he tilted the tip over with his thumbs in one direction and another, then he put his left hand on top and pushed down, and the whole whirling and spinning column collapsed into a squat, round mound under his long, tapering fingers.

Now his motion changed. He squeezed the sponge into the bucket again, brought another inundation of water onto the round, smooth lump on the wheel, then cupped both his hands around the clay. His thumbs met on top, in the middle of the clay. They pushed down, dug in, pulled outwards to hollow (muck spun off the wheel, splattered everything in a circle around it, dripped off his apron down onto his boots). His foot kicked the wheel again, ten, twelve fast, hard kicks, then went back to brace itself against the support bar.

Another squeeze of the sponge. Guy shifted his position, tipping his head so he looked at the piece sideways. His hair fell over his eyes; he shook it back and pushed one wavy red strand out of his face with the back of his hand, leaving a smear of clay unnoticed across his forehead. He gave the wheel another few kicks and put his fingers in place on the inside and outside of the beginning pot.

Gently, smoothly, in front of Cat's astonished eyes, whirling and spinning, a vessel rose under his hands. One upward pull of the knuckles, two, a third one, and a perfect cup was revolving on the wheel.

But Guy's motion did not stop. He reached for the sponge again, squeezed it dry, then sponged away the soft watery slurry that coated the vessel and wheel surface. Inside the cup and out, the sponge marked fine ridges in the clay. He squeezed the slurry into the bucket, rinsed the sponge, wiped another bit of slip off the wheel, then exchanged the sponge for a wooden tool, flat and pointed on one end like the tip of a kitchen knife.

Inserting it into the angle between the cup and the wheel, he scraped away a wedge of the clay at the foot of the piece. He dropped the tool back into the jar and reached for the cutting wire. His foot braked the flywheel to a stop;

he tightened the wire between his hands and drew it across the wheelhead, slicing the cup off the wheel.

Cat broke into spontaneous applause, and Guy looked up and grinned his crooked grin at her.

"It's not that amazing, once you've seen it a few times." He cupped his flat hands around the vessel and very gently lifted it off the wheel to the shelf in front of him.

"Well, it's amazing to me!" Cat said. "I could watch this forever. It's such a soothing motion, organic, like it's growing. Do you enjoy doing that?"

"Yes, I do," he said, smacking a second piece of clay into the centre of the wheelhead and kicking the wheel into motion. "I like the way the clay feels under my hands, how it moves and responds to what I do. And unlike some,"—a quick shadow passed over his face—"I don't mind the muck." He bent over the wheel again and started centring the clay.

Cat smiled. "No, I wouldn't either. I still walk barefoot in the mud if I have a chance, I like the squishiness between my toes."

He gave her a quick, upwards glance, surprised, questioning, then silently he turned back to his work.

They spent the next hour in companionable silence. Cat watched Guy as he made a dozen cups to replace the ones he'd discarded. When she got tired of watching, she collected a chair from the cottage and sat at the table, playing with the piece of clay she had tried to wedge.

She dug her fingers into it, twisted it, rolled it, poked it, squished it, and then without really meaning to she had made a small sculpture, stuck on the end of her raised index finger. It looked like a little head, a gnome, grinning at her mischievously. She grinned back at it, enjoying what she had made.

"Nice," said Guy over her shoulder.

She looked up at him standing behind her. He certainly was tall, she thought; she had to tip her head right back to look up at his face.

"Stick it on the drying shelf," he said. "We can fire it with the other stuff." He limped over to the shelf and took a rag from a hook on its side.

"What? Oh, nah. I was just fooling around."

"No, it's a nice little piece. If you really don't want it fired when it's dry, you can reuse the clay later." He went back to the wheel, scraped the stuck-on clay off with a spatula, then ran the rag around the edge of the wheelhead where the wet slurry had accumulated in a thick round of sludge.

"Well, if you think so..."

"I do. I'm just going to wash these off." He gestured at her with a handful of clay-covered tools, then threw them in his water bucket and limped out the door with it. Cat heard him rattling the pump handle outside.

She looked at the gnome head on her finger.

"Hmph. You're no beauty," she told it. "But if the potter thinks we should keep you, I guess keep you we will." She pried it off her finger, and it came loose with a soft little *shlumpf.* "There, now your ear is squished. Oh well." She took it to the drying shelf and found it a spot where the cups had been, then stepped back to look at it from a different angle.

She stopped in surprise.

There was a hollow *thump* where her foot hit the floorboards. What was that? She tapped her foot again, and then again a little bit over. Solid here. Back one step, hollow.

Was there another storage space under there? This was easily two yards over from where Guy had taken out the oilcloth-wrapped lump; that space couldn't extend this far—could it?

Cat squatted down and inspected the floorboards. Rapping her knuckles on the wood, she found that the hollow-sounding part here was small, only about one by two feet. She couldn't see a knothole like the one Guy had used to pull up the other trap door.

But there! There was a little indentation, shallow enough to escape notice if you weren't specifically looking for it. Cat pushed her finger into the notch, and it tipped down, pivoting up another section of the board about a foot away.

As suspected, another trap door!

Cat slipped her fingers under the raised edge of the board and lifted it up.

In the depths of the hole, sparkling up at Cat with an eerie, iridescent shimmer, rested three turquoise bowls.

CHAPTER 15

T URQUOISE BOWLS.

Cat started back, averting her gaze.

But out of the corner of her eye she could still see them, shimmering, gleaming. And the workshop was solid—there was no whirling and swirling, no dancing and spinning that was pulling her into the bowls.

She dared a look, sideways at first, then full-on, right into the depths of the pots.

Nothing happened.

The room around Cat remained perfectly still, and she breathed a sigh of relief.

She bent closer, letting the trap door over the hole fall back to stay open on its own.

The bowls were beautiful. Two of them were stacked together, roughly the same size; the lower one had sides that sloped outward with a gently flared lip, the other was wide and round-bellied, its rim narrowing and then flaring out again, the upper edge delicate and thin.

And the third—Cat drew a sharp breath. The third was the exact match to the bowl that had pulled her from the museum and whirled her into this country. The twin of that bowl, nestling under the floor of the potter's workshop.

Cat cautiously reached out a hand. Would it be safe to touch? Could she...?

She stretched her fingers, reached...

"NO!!" bellowed a voice behind her.

Cat whirled around.

Guy burst through the door, his face white and contorted, his turquoise eyes blazing with fury.

"Do not DARE touch those!" he screamed, lunging towards her.

Cat threw up her hands in terror and stumbled backwards. *Screaming—Filthy temper—Killed her—KILLED HER!!*

Hot fear raced over her body, her throat closed up in panic, tears shot into her eyes. Her back met the wood slats of the drying shelf, and she flung out a hand to steady herself.

"No, no, don't!" she forced out through a choking voice, her arm raised to ward off the blow she was certain would fall.

But none came.

Cat drew a sobbing breath; her heart was racing so hard that her whole body pulsed with it. She blinked rapidly.

The thrumming in her head slowed, the red haze of fear over her vision gradually receded.

Now she saw that Guy was holding onto the table where he had caught himself as his leg gave out; he gripped the edge so hard his knuckles showed white. His eyes, huge in his deathly pale face, stared at Cat for a few interminable seconds.

Then his whole body went limp.

"Please," his voice was a hoarse whisper, "*please* do not touch those bowls!" He staggered and blindly reached out behind him, searching for support. His hand met the chair, and he dropped down onto it. He threw his hand over his eyes. "*Please,*" he repeated, brokenly.

Cat was trembling, but her rapid heartbeat gradually slowed, and she was able to blink back her tears.

Cautiously, she let go of the support of the shelf and lowered her hands, but she kept them spread in front of her to show that she wasn't trying to touch anything. Nothing. Especially not any turquoise bowls.

She stepped sideways, giving the open trapdoor a wide berth.

"Okay," she said shakily, "okay." (*Smooth, Cat. That's the way to talk to a killer.*) "Guy? It's okay. I'm not touching."

He drew a ragged breath, keeping his hand over his face.

"Guy? I didn't know. Okay? I didn't know."

Guy drew his hand down his face and pinched the bridge of his nose. Not meeting Cat's eyes, he said, "No. No, you didn't."

Cat leaned against the table, carefully studying the way her fingertips, still trembling slightly, ran over the weave of the canvas covering.

"Guy—*what* is it I didn't know?"

He shook his head.

"*They* didn't know either," he said in a low voice that Cat could barely hear, "and it didn't help them." His eyes were bleak, staring blindly at the floor of the workshop, his head turned away from the storage hole with the turquoise bowls.

Cat took a deep breath and felt the adrenaline slowly settle out in her body. This was no longer a deranged killer. Here was a man as much in need of her help as when he had lain unconscious in the forest, as much as when in his agony he had crushed her hand.

Besides, he owed her an explanation.

Cat fished under the worktable for a stool that she had seen there earlier, and sat herself down across the corner of the table from Guy.

"All right," she said, her voice gentle, her eyes on his face. "Tell me."

Once again he shook his head, hopelessly.

"I don't think I can make you understand," he said. "I don't really understand myself."

"For starters, you can just fill me in," Cat said. "For example, who are 'they'? You said 'they didn't know, either'—who did you mean?"

His voice continued low, broken.

"My—my wife. And my brother. Sepp. The—the Septimissimus."

Cat nodded,

"I thought as much. I heard—" She broke off, wishing she had kept her mouth shut.

His head came up.

"What did you hear?"

"Well, there was a girl," Cat said reluctantly, "in the village. Your wife's cousin?"

He gave a cynical snort.

"Dear Kashinka. I wonder what she had to say. She probably thinks I murdered them both."

Oh dear. Cat drew patterns on the canvas table top with her fingernail.

"Does she? She does." He gave a harsh laugh. "I wonder how I'm supposed to have done it? Oh no, she's found me out." He reached for one of the lumps of clay that still lay on the table, and his long, powerful fingers wrapped themselves around it. "I strangled my wife. With my bare hands." He squeezed and the clay constricted, the top bulging out over his hand, until it fell off with a sickening *plop.*

"As for my brother," he continued with a mad gleam in his eyes, snatching up the cutting wire from among the tools flung on the table and snapping it taut between his hands, "his neck is a little thicker, it took something extra."

He dropped the wire and let his hands sink into his lap. "Of course, there are other methods," he mused. "The clay pit—it's so easy to drown in, all that sticky clay..." He picked up the lump of clay he had decapitated, pressed it back together, then squished it with his right hand onto his flattened left. The clay oozed out between his splayed fingers. "It doesn't even take a whole clay pit—one lump is enough, pushed over the nose and mouth..."

He slapped his flat hand with the clay onto the table, making Cat jump.

"But, no, it was none of those!" he cried. He waved a clay-stained forefinger at Cat. "The glazes! I used my glazes! There is some quite toxic stuff in my glaze cupboard, you know. Poisoning is such a clean method to dispose of someone." He leaned forward conversationally on his elbows, looking at Cat as if he were simply telling her a gossipy piece of news. "And speaking of clean disposing, there's of course the bodies to get rid of. But nothing could be simpler when you have a kiln. All that's left after firing is a little pile of ashes."

He leaned back in the chair and crossed his arms over his chest.

"So you see," his lip curled, bitter, cynical, "Kashinka isn't far off. I could have murdered them—oh so easily."

Oh really. Cat was getting fed up with the histrionics. For a moment, she had almost believed he was serious.

She looked him straight in the face, her eyes holding his turquoise ones, issuing a challenge.

"And did you?"

"Murder them?" His eyes dropped and his shoulders slumped. There was nothing left of his artificial cockiness, only bleak brokenness. "I might as well have."

CHAPTER 16

"So suppose," Catriona said, "you really start at the beginning. I don't know a whole lot of what's going on here, you know. There's you, there's your brother, and there's your wife. And Bibby, but we'll leave her out for the moment. Let's start with your wife."

"Ashya." Guy spoke the name in a flat tone, as if he was trying to ward himself off from whatever feelings it had once evoked in him.

"All right, Ashya. How long were you married?"

"Two years. It would be three now, except... Well. She is—was—very beautiful; you've seen her cousin, she's a lot like her. Except Ashya was fair, not dark."

"How did you meet?"

"In the village; we both grew up here."

Of course, that was a dumb question. But at least it kept him talking.

"Were you, you know, childhood sweethearts or something?"

He raised his eyebrows and shook his head. "Uh, no. She's quite a bit younger than me. I didn't pay much attention to her; she was just a child. But she grew up to be—quite beautiful. And then suddenly, she decided that, for whatever reason, she wanted me. Or at least that she wanted to be married to me, goodness knows why. I guess she thought I was something important, something—something I was not. *Am* not." He rubbed his hand over his forehead. "That can be the only reason, because..." He let his gaze travel around the workshop. "Well, she was good at wanting things. And she wanted to marry me, so we married. She was just eighteen then. She was beautiful," he repeated, as if that explained everything.

Cat decided she couldn't stand this woman.

"What do you mean about her thinking you were something different than you are?"

"It must be that," Guy said. "Else why would she want to marry me?"

Cat wasn't going to answer that. She didn't know him nearly well enough to make personal remarks of that kind.

"It certainly wasn't that she wanted to live here." He gestured at the pottery wheel. "She hated it."

Ah, that comment earlier about the muck and mess of pottery. Cat knew there had been something behind that.

"But she married you anyway. And wasn't happy?"

"No. Like I said, she was good at wanting things, and not good at putting up with not getting them. She always wanted more, wanted what I couldn't give her. Wanted to move back to town, wanted a larger and better house, couldn't understand why I wouldn't fall in with her ideas. My work requires me to be close to where the clay is, where I can run the kiln!"

"Of course," Cat said. "That goes without saying."

He gave a humourless laugh. "It didn't for her. I sometimes think she expected me to be giving up pottery altogether. I don't know what gave her that idea. I'm a craftsman, my work is who I am. And besides, what other income do I have? But then, I don't know what gave her any of her ideas—I never understood her."

"That can't have been easy."

There was that cynical twist to his mouth again. "It was all right at first. If she got what she wanted she was happy for a little while, and like I said, she wanted to marry me. I sometimes had the feeling she was waiting for something, was expecting something to happen. And then something did happen—but not what she wanted."

"Bibby," Cat guessed.

Guy nodded.

"*Definitely* not what she wanted. I suppose—I suppose being pregnant is... Well, she was miserable. She hated how it changed her body, hated how it tied her down. I thought it would be all right once the babe was born, that it would give her something to do, that she would like being a mother. But it just got worse. She didn't like giving the babe the breast, hated the diapers, loathed the crying. I tried to do what I could, but I had my work to do, and I couldn't do both at once. But, I didn't understand, I still don't understand... Bibby—how could she not love her?"

The pain in his voice was so raw, Cat had to swallow past a lump. She cleared her throat and made an effort to speak calmly.

"So then what happened?"

"One day it came to a head. Bibby was small, seven or eight months. I had a big order to fill, and I was running low on clay, so I went to the pit to get more. I suppose I should have paid closer attention, should have realized that Ashya—that she was unhappy—but then she was always unhappy... If I had noticed it, had tried to give her more space that day, perhaps then..."

"What did she do?"

"She wanted to go to town, to the market. Do some shopping at the vendors' that had come from the city for the summer fair. And so she just went."

"What do you mean, she just went?"

"She walked out of the house. Without Bibby."

"What??"

He nodded. "Yes. Bibby was having a nap, and I suppose Ashya thought she'd keep sleeping. Or that she'd keep herself entertained when she woke up. Or—really, I suppose Ashya didn't think at all. She didn't, not usually."

Cat gave a small huff. Unbelievable. "And then?"

"I came back with my clay buckets, and it seemed unusually quiet in the cottage. So I looked. And there was the babe crawling around on the floor, four inches away from the fire."

Cat gasped, and Guy nodded.

"If I had been even two seconds later, she would have been right in the coals," he said grimly. "I suppose I was... angry."

"Uh, yeah!"

"I grabbed the babe, and I went after Ashya. I found her in town at a haberdasher's stall, choosing ribbon colours.

While her child was a hair's breadth away from burning to death!"

"What did you do?"

He twisted his mouth ruefully. "I lost my temper. I—I do have a temper."

Cat bit back a snort. *You don't say.*

"And...?"

"I don't remember what I said—or shouted, rather. I know I should have controlled myself better... I made her come home with me. She wasn't happy."

"I bet."

"And that's when she told me she was divorcing me. Leaving for good. I tried to argue, tried to get her to stay, for Bibby's sake, but she was adamant. I... We... She said things... how I was—was..." He dropped his forehead into his palms. "She screamed that she was leaving, over and over... And then she broke the marriage chain."

Cat stood up and moved across the room. He looked up at her now, as she went to the carved cupboard, squatted down, and reached into the bottom shelf. She came back to the table and presented her open palm to him.

"Was this hers?" she asked.

An expression of sadness crossed his face as he looked down at the tarnished, mangled silver bird. He picked it up and closed his hand around it.

"Yes. That was her marriage chain. I couldn't bear it anymore, the shouting and screaming. Bibby was crying her heart out, so I picked her up and turned my back on Ashya and walked in here. She came after me and she tore off the chain, snapped it, and flung it away; I never knew

127

where it landed. And I didn't have the heart to look for it, later, when it was all over."

Cat sat back down. She leaned her elbows on the table and put her chin in her hands.

"And then?"

A slight shudder ran over his frame.

"And then she saw the bowls," he said quietly. "Those bowls." He awkwardly got up from his chair and limped over to the open trap door. He frowned down at the turquoise dishes for a moment, then tipped the trap door shut with his foot. "They had only come out of the kiln that morning and sat on the table, barely cooled off. There were five of them then; one had broken in the kiln, but there were two complete pairs left, and one single one. I've never had a glaze like that before, ever, and I still don't know what made it come out like that, let alone whether I could repeat it. Not that I'd want to, after what happened." He dropped back down into the chair.

Cat's eyes were fixed on his face.

"What did happen?"

"Ashya saw the bowls, and she stopped dead. She was like that—she'd see something, and suddenly want it, and that was that."

"They *are* beautiful."

He shook his head. "No, it wasn't that. There is—there is something about them that—that... I think Ashya saw it, knew it—she was an Unissima, you know—"

"Yes, Ouska said."

Guy made a huffing noise. "She did? She would. She never liked Ashya, you know."

The corner of Cat's mouth twitched. "I got that impression, yes. So, Ashya..."

"Ashya wanted the bowls. And she put out her hand, and she took one, and she was gone."

"What do you mean, gone? Not—dead?"

"No, gone. Vanished. Disappeared. And so was the bowl. One moment they were here, and the next they weren't. *And I don't know where they went.* Ashya probably *is* dead, for all I know." He fell silent.

"Hmm," Cat said. Her own experience with one such bowl would say otherwise. "I doubt it."

Guy jerked his shoulder in a hopeless shrug.

"All right, so that's your wife. Then what happened?"

He gave her a questioning look.

Cat shook her head impatiently.

"Your brother? What happened with him?"

"Sepp." Guy gave an affectionate snort. "My *little* brother." With a grin he held up his hand at the level of his nose to show just how short that brother was, then he suddenly sobered and pressed his lips together. A muscle jumped in his cheek.

"He's younger than you?" Cat already knew the answer, but she wanted to get him talking again.

"Yes, we're the youngest in the family. We were always together. There's five brothers ahead of us, and two sisters—like I said, the Septimissimus. Seventh son of the Seventh Septimus. Aunt tell you that, too?"

Cat nodded.

"We always knew that, of course, about him being the Septimissimus. It never made any difference to us—why should it?"

So much for that Kashinka's "filthy jealous".

"What's he like?"

"Oh, he's a silly fool—likes to joke around, that sort of thing. Cheerful. I'm the dull one who always wants to think things over. He calls me Master Dark-and-Gloom. But then, he was coming up on twenty-eight, and you know what that means..."

"What what means?"

"Aunt didn't tell you? The Seventh Septimus or the Septimissimus. When he turns twenty-eight (four for the seasons and the times of the day, and seven for the number of the sons), that's when his powers come into full force."

"Oh, that's connected to age? Does it matter if his father is still alive? Ouska said that with an Unissima—"

"No, it doesn't matter. An Unissima is different, she's a woman, for one."

Cat laughed.

"Yes, I had figured out that much!"

His crooked grin flashed out, then disappeared again.

"As I was *saying*," he repeated with emphasis, "*unlike* an Unissima, for the Septimissimus it's the twenty-eighth birthday that matters. For the full powers, that is; there's usually something you can see before then, it sort of builds to it. And what was building with Sepp was his temper. Or it was changing, anyway. He got more and more—well, I suppose 'morose' is the best word. Just in a mood. Angry, snappish. Turning into Master Dark-and-Gloom himself.

That isn't like him—*wasn't* like him." He fell silent, sadness descending on his face.

"Go on," prompted Cat gently, as much to pull him out of his despondence as to find out what happened.

"We were all waiting for something to happen, for his powers to show. The day after his birthday—yes, Friday, I think—he came around here—"

"Wait, so you didn't meet him in the town? Ouska said you did."

"I don't think—oh yes, you're right, I did. I had gone in to deliver an order to someone. Saw Sepp on the street, and he didn't even say hello to Bibby. Snapped at her when she pulled on his sleeve to get his attention, the idiot. So I told him what I thought of that kind of behaviour, and went home."

That didn't exactly sound like a screaming match in the streets—a disagreement, nothing more.

"And then?"

"He came after me, an hour or so later, to apologize. He's really fond of Bibby and usually spoils her rotten, so he felt bad that he'd made her cry. But, see, that's just it, he'd never do a thing like that normally, and if he did it wouldn't take him an hour to make up. He was just not himself!"

"Did you find what was wrong?"

"Eventually. It took some digging and prodding, and some kisses from Bibby (they're slobbery)." His mouth quirked up on one corner. "And about two cups of Uncle's applejack. Turns out Sepp is—*was*—worried about his powers. I didn't know, but he'd never been particularly confident in them. I mean, we all knew he was the One, and his powers would just come when he was twenty-eight."

"Does that bother you, him being so special, I mean, and you just his brother?" Cat thought she knew the answer to that one, but she wanted to hear him say it.

He looked at her in surprise.

"Why would it? It's not like it's any particular privilege. If anything, it can be a burden to bear, a responsibility. I sometimes think Sepp would be—would have been—glad to be rid of it, but it's his gift, and so he needs to use it. We all have our gifts, and they're there to serve others. At least that's what *most* of us think." He had that cynical twist to his mouth again; Cat knew he was thinking of his wife.

"So he worried about his powers."

"He thought he'd ruined it all. Spoiled his powers. First, with hankering after a life 'out there'—he wanted to know what else there was, in the world beyond Ruph. We sometimes talked of it, ever since we were little, of what lies beyond our village and our valley; but I was content with talking of it, while he wanted to go and see for himself. But we knew that he couldn't, that his place was here. The Septimissimus is needed, he cannot just go wherever he pleases. But that wasn't all. You see—you know that rocking chair?" He gestured in the direction of the cottage.

"Yes, of course. I did spend a whole night it in."

He gave her a quick, sidelong glance, questioning. *Oh,* Cat thought, *I suppose he was unconscious, he wouldn't know.*

"So, what about the rocking chair?"

"If you've sat in it, you'll know it's an, uh, *unusual* piece of furniture."

"Yes?"

"*Sepp made it.*"

Cat had the feeling she was missing something.

"Uh... okay?"

"He's the Septimissimus! He's not supposed to be a craftsman!"

"Oh!" Right, Ouska had mentioned something of the sort. "So, why did he?"

"It's like he couldn't help himself. He's done it ever since we were little, picked up bits of wood, stuck them together, whittled them into different shapes, that sort of thing. He got better and better at it."

"Sounds like he's a natural at it."

Guy rubbed his hand over the back of his neck. "I didn't know that I should stop him. At first I didn't even notice—I was just a little kid myself, and I didn't know why anyone would choose sticks over clay when clay is so much nicer. But you know brothers, they're odd." He flashed his brief grin again. "Then when we were maybe five and six, one day I suddenly got to wondering why our father didn't have a trade or a craft like all his brothers. I went and asked Uncle about it (he and Aunt always had time for us, more than our parents did with their nine children and the Septimus work). And Uncle told me."

Cat thought of her library storytime kids. "Six is pretty little. Did you understand what he was talking about?"

"Well enough. Like I said, we grew up with the knowledge of it all, it wasn't a far stretch. So, once I got it through my head that Sepp wouldn't be able to be a craftsman, I tried to make him stop. We had a few rows about it. I took away a little toy rocking horse he'd carved, and another time I broke a tiny chair he made. He got back at me by smashing my very best pinch pot, and we both ended up with bloody noses." He chuckled.

"*Of course they fought,*" Cat heard Ouska's voice in her head, "*they're brothers, aren't they?*"

"He didn't stop though, did he?" she said aloud.

Guy shook his head. "No. I realized pretty quickly—rather surprising for the age I was—that is was pointless to try to make him. And I didn't know how serious it was. I was only a kid!"

"Of course. So what did you do?"

"I worked on hiding what he was doing. It took me a while to make him understand, but once he did, he only did his woodwork where nobody but me saw him. And I hid his projects. In fact, once we were older and I started apprenticing as potter, I used most of them for firing the kiln when my master wasn't looking."

Cat gasped. "You *burned* your brother's work?"

He shrugged. "It wasn't supposed to exist in the first place. And that way he could keep making things from wood without it causing trouble. We just didn't have room to keep it anymore; he'd moved on to making full-sized pieces of furniture by then. Besides, I didn't destroy his pieces entirely. Well, yes, they burned up, but I saved the ashes, and when the pottery became my own, I used them for glazes. Or I used to, before—" He stopped.

"Before what?"

He took a deep breath. "Before Ashya. Once she was in the cottage, we didn't dare anymore. We couldn't have her knowing about it; who knows what she would have done if she found out."

Cat could just imagine.

"It was too bad, too," Guy said. "The glazes from his furniture ashes were the best I had, apart from—" His gaze slid to the trap door that hid the turquoise bowls. "All my other ones are just brown."

"Are those the pots in the bottom of the cupboard? Greens and blues, really different from your other pots?"

"Yes. That's why they're in there. I didn't want anyone asking questions. You see, the thing is, probably because it was Sepp's work that made those ashes, there was something, well, different about them, and so the glazes from them also came out differently."

That kind of made sense.

"So when did he stop making furniture?"

"That's just it, he didn't. He started on that rocking chair when Bibby was born, for Ashya to rock her to sleep in. I don't know if you noticed, but it has a bird carved in the back rest; that bird was supposed to be for my wife, like the bird on her wedding chain. I have no idea how we would have kept her from finding out it was Sepp's work—if nothing else, her Knowing should have told her. I guess neither of us thought about it. But as it was, by the time the chair was finished, the bird was Bibby, anyone could see that; and Ashya was gone. She never did use that chair."

Now why should that little fact make Cat feel smug?

"So you kept the chair."

"Yes. I suppose I should have put it in the fire, but I couldn't bear to. So I kept it."

"I'm glad," Cat said.

Guy looked up and gave her a surprised smile, then he shrugged one shoulder.

"It's not as if anyone ever comes here to see it," he said. "In fact—huh, if you've sat in it, you're the first person to do so other than me. And Bibby of course. And Sepp. He's really good at—" His voice cracked. "He *was* really good at rocking her."

Cat's eyes prickled, and she blinked.

"So what happened?"

He swallowed and swiped the heel of his hand at the corner of his eye.

"Sepp was worried that because he'd broken the rules and done a craftsman's work, he'd squandered his Septimus powers. As I said, we always knew he would get his powers at twenty-eight, but he turned twenty-eight last week, and nothing happened. At least he didn't think anything had happened."

"Exactly what were you expecting?"

"We didn't know just *what* was supposed to happen. If the onset of powers would be gradual or sudden, if he would know, if others would know, if anyone would see it or he would feel it, or what. Our father passed on more than two years ago, so we couldn't ask him, and there wasn't a Septimus for decades before him."

"So nobody knew."

"No. And Sepp worried that he'd ruined the Septimissimus gift, had spoiled his powers by using another gift instead."

"Goodness, that sounds awful."

Guy made a scoffing sound. "Yes. Well, that was bad enough. By then the applejack really hit him—if that's what did it, I don't know. He started talking nonsense like I'd never heard him before. He was worthless and totally devoid of a gift at all, and he wouldn't know one anyway, not if it jumped up and bit him, and he was a complete loss to the community and the world as a whole and he might as well take himself off and never come back. I wanted to shake him. But I knew that wouldn't help, and I didn't know what to tell him."

Cat nodded. "So what did you do?"

His brows drew together.

"The worst thing I could have done."

"Oh?"

"I'd never told him exactly what happened to my wife. He knew it had something to do with me, with what I did."

How did he figure that? From what Cat had heard, that woman had pretty much only herself to blame.

"Sepp thought she'd left this town, gone to the city or something. But with the mood he was in... I thought if I told him the truth, maybe it would snap him out of it. Maybe he'd see that his imaginary failure—which we didn't even know if it was a failure or not—was really nothing compared to my gigantic one..."

There was something seriously screwed up about his way of thinking. "So you told him what happened?"

Guy groaned.

"Worse. Much, much worse. Oh stars, the fool I was!"

Well, yes, perhaps, though not quite in the way he thought.

"So..."

"I took him in here, and I brought out the bowls."

"What?"

"Oh, I can touch them. Nothing happens to *me* when I pick them up, I've tried often enough. I took one of those bowls out, and I put it on the table, and I told Sepp what I had done to my wife. I told my brother—" His voice dropped, and he swallowed hard. "I told my brother what happened to Ashya. I turned around to get out the other bowls, and—and..." His voice broke.

Cat laid her hand on his arm. "And he picked up the bowl?"

Guy nodded, staring bleakly in front of him.

"I—I turned around," he said haltingly, "and just saw him do it. He took it, and he was gone. Just—just like her." He pressed his hand over his eyes. "My doing. Both of them. Mine. My fault. They're gone, they're dead..."

Cat was silent.

Then she took a deep breath.

It was time to tell him.

CHAPTER 17

"**G**uy?" Cat began, "Guy, I—I don't think they're dead."

He raised his head and stared at her.

"In fact, I'm quite sure of it. You see, I—well, the place where I come from—"

Guy frowned, grief vying with bewilderment on his face. "Where you...?"

"I think I'm from another world entirely," Cat said. "But actually, it's not so much where, it's how."

The frown deepened, and he drew a breath to speak.

"No, just listen. I was sort of, well, dropped, in the forest here—the Wald, I guess you call it. One minute I was in my world, and the next I was here." Cat rubbed her forehead. When you said it like this, it really sounded crazy. "And then Bibby came, except I didn't know she was Bibby then, and we went and found you..." (*Way to go, Cat, now you sound completely demented. Stop babbling and get to the point.*) She took another deep breath and brought it out in a rush.

"...and I think it was one of your bowls that did it!"

Guy reared back.

"What??"

"I was in—in a museum, it's a place where they show stuff, old dishes and things. And there was a bowl, just like these ones." She pointed at the trap door. "In fact, it was *exactly* like one of those."

He sprang to his feet, then had to catch himself on the table for balance. More cautiously, he moved to the trap door, squatted down, and opened it. He reached into the hole and brought out the pot-bellied bowl.

"This one?"

"No, the other one, the one that was sitting by itself, not stacked with this one."

Guy took one of the remaining two bowls out and set it on the floor beside the open trap door.

"Yes, that one." Cat pointed. "The one with the rounded top."

"Sepp's. That was the bowl that Sepp picked up." He sounded completely bewildered. "So where is it now?"

"I have no idea. Presumably still back there, in Greenward Falls in the museum. I never even touched it. I just—"

"Wait, so what—how—*what* happened?"

Poor man, he was completely confused. Not that she could blame him; she was making a total hash of telling the story.

"I'm sorry, I'll start over. I was in a museum."

"All right…" He looked at her, his brow contracting in concentration.

"There was a display case," Cat gestured with her hands to show its size and shape, "and inside it with some other things was a bowl, just like that one."

"Yes..." Guy slowly nodded his understanding.

"I bent over it and looked at it, and then it—I don't know, it pulled me into it. I can't explain it better than that. Everything swirled around me in circles, and all of a sudden I was here. In the forest."

He shook his head, a puzzled frown on his face. "It pulled you into..."

Suddenly there came sounds from the cottage.

"Hello!" called a woman's voice. "Anyone here? Where are you?"

Guy clambered to his feet and moved around so his body hid the bowls on the floor.

The door between the cottage and workshop creaked open, and Yldra's head appeared around the door.

"There you are! I've brought Bibby home. She's had a busy day, she's tired. So how's my favourite cousin? I hear you banged your head and poked a hole in your leg, and it needed Mother, Father, *and* our new friend here to patch you up." She winked at Cat.

"Hmph," snorted Guy, limping over to the door, "at least they didn't get *your* help with it, or I'd still be flat on my back in bed."

With practised ease he ducked his head out of the way as she took a swipe at him, and sidled past her into the cottage.

"Cousins!" Yldra said to Cat with a grin and an eye roll. "You got any of those? They can be a right pest!"

"No, not a one. Nor brother or sister. I wish I did."

"An only child, are you? Interesting." The young woman gave Cat a searching look that was strongly reminiscent of her mother. Then she lowered her voice. "Catriona, how is he?" She tipped her head in the direction of the open cottage door.

"Better, I think," Cat replied in the same tone. "At least physically. I mean, I hardly know him, so I don't know..."

"Yes, that's all that can be expected these days," Yldra said, her eyes a little sad. "He's not been the same since... Ah well."

"You're close?"

"Closer than with my own brothers. They're a lot older than me." She moved towards the door. "And were a lot nicer to me, too!" she added in a loud voice as she stepped through into the cottage.

Guy, who sat on the bench by the table with Bibby on his good knee, looked up at that.

"Who was nicer?"

Bibby spotted Cat, who came into the cottage after Yldra, and pointed. "Gah!" she called happily, looking up at her father to see if he quite understood how delightful this meeting was. Cat smiled back at her.

"Yes, that's Cat," Guy said. "Who was nicer to you, coz?"

"My brothers. Much nicer than you and Sepp." Yldra laid her hand on her stomach with a small smile. "I hope this one will draw a better lot with her playmates."

Guy's eyebrows rose, and his mouth pursed into a whistle.

"Ooooh, that's the way it is, is it?" His crooked grin looked pleased. "Young Randor had better look out. If his baby sister turns out anything like his mother, he'll have to fight for his rights, like we did."

Yldra patted Guy consolingly on the top of the head, which she could only reach because he was sitting down.

"You poor, poor things. I was so hard on you, wasn't I. Bullied and bossed you within an inch of your lives, and you had no way to defend yourself, being a mere four years older and boys at that."

"Too true, alas," Guy said with a mournful shake of his head. "It was awful."

"Well, I've made it up to you today by bringing you some more bread and cheese from Mother. But you'll have to make your own mintbrew. Father thinks you're well enough now to boil the kettle, which is just as well as poor Catriona won't want to deal with your primitive cooking facilities."

"I wouldn't know how," Cat said with a smile.

"I don't blame you," Yldra said. "I could do it, but I wouldn't want to. And I have to get home to my own poor defenseless boys." She ruffled Bibby's curls. "I'll leave you to it for now."

"She's really nice," said Cat as the door closed behind Yldra. "Do you have any other cousins?"

"Oh yes, about three or four dozen," Guy replied carelessly. "Half the town is related to us. Eew!" He quickly put Bibby on the floor. "Wet drawers!" He rubbed at a spot on his breeches.

Cat laughed and took the little girl around to the privy to finish her business.

By the time they came back and she got clean, dry clothes on the baby again, Guy had stoked the fire. A black iron bar, shaped like an upside-down L, was swung out from the side of the fireplace, and a heavy black cast-iron kettle hung from one of the strong hooks that were attached to the horizontal bar.

Cat was surprised she hadn't noticed the bar before. It must swing right inside the fireplace when it wasn't in use. No wonder Yldra had been so dismissive of the cooking facilities here; she probably had one of those nice closed stoves like her mother.

Guy took a potholder, lifted the kettle from the hook, and looked inside it.

"Not enough water," he said, and went out to the pump.

When he came back, Cat could tell the kettle was heavy; his limp was quite pronounced.

"I could have done that," she said. "Your leg looks like it hurts."

He waved aside her concern.

"It's all right," he said. "I can handle it." He hung the kettle on its hook and used a long poker to swing the crane back into the fireplace so the kettle hung over the flame.

"Guy," said Cat, a little hesitantly, "your leg, couldn't you, well, cure it?"

Guy tipped his head to the side with a questioning frown.

She held out her hand, opening and closing her fist.

"See, yesterday morning, when you squeezed my hand, you pretty much crushed it. I suppose it comes from all that clay squishing you do. I thought every bone in that hand was broken."

He winced. "I'm so sorry."

"No, no, that's not what I mean! It's okay! It's totally okay now!" She wiggled her fingers like she was playing an arpeggio.

Guy's eyes widened, and he breathed a sigh of relief.

"You made my hand well again," Cat continued, "when you held it. What did you do then? I mean, you just cured it, totally healed it. It doesn't hurt at all how, there's no sign anything ever happened to it, let alone as recently as yesterday. Not a twinge. Can't you do that with your leg?"

He pulled a rueful grimace.

"No, I can't," he said, rubbing his hand over the back of his neck. "I'm really glad your hand is better. It's not the first time it happened, that instant cure, but there was only one other time. I've tried, when the babe hurt herself, and even when I've done something to myself, which happens a lot."

"Does it?"

"I'm very clumsy. At least have been in the last year or so. I'm always tripping and cutting myself and dropping things. I've got plenty of cuts and bruises and scars to show for it."

"Ouch. But how do you manage then?"

He shrugged. "They're mostly small hurts. This one"—he rubbed at his leg above the injury—"was rather worse than most. But as with all the others, I'll just have to wait for it to heal."

"What was different about my hand then?"

Guy slowly shook his head. "I don't know. Not really. I have a guess... You see, the other time, the first time it happened, it was Bibby. And it was my carelessness that caused it."

"What happened?"

"She was just barely walking. I was unloading the kiln, and as usual I was too impatient to wait until the wares had cooled down. I'm always itching to know how the glazes turned out, so I unload when they're still so hot I have to use tongs to handle them. And I hadn't properly closed the door to the house, I was in such a rush. So out Bibby toddled when my back was turned, and tried to pick up one of the steaming hot pots."

Cat drew in a hissing breath. "Oh no!"

"Oh yes." He nodded grimly. "I don't think I'll ever forget those screams."

"What did you do?"

"I snatched her up and ran to the pump for cold water, holding her poor little hands in mine—all I wanted, with every fibre of my being, was to make it somehow better—and then she suddenly stopped crying. Just like that. Stopped crying, and smiled at me. I almost dropped her, I was so surprised." He chuckled weakly. "Her hands were perfectly well, not a blister, not even any more red than usual. And she acted as if nothing happened."

"Oh my gosh!" Cat let out a breath she hadn't known she was holding. She scooped up Bibby from the bench and hugged her tight, just to relieve her own feelings. The little girl squeaked, and Cat hurriedly put her down again.

"Sorry, sweetie," she said. "But, wow, that must have been scary!"

"It was," Guy said.

"So, does it only work on hands, then, the healing?"

"No," he said thoughtfully. "When Bibby slammed her finger in the lid of the chest the next day, I had to kiss it better the old-fashioned way. As for myself, I'm always getting cuts and bruises all over my hands, and the only thing that does a little good for them is Aunt's ointments." He turned his long-fingered hand over and rubbed his thumb over some small scars on the back of his knuckles.

"You said you had a guess though."

"Yes. I think... I think it has something to do with how the hurt came about. See," his turquoise gaze locked with Cat's, "both your hand and Bibby's, it was my doing. My fault. Perhaps when I hurt someone, even if I don't mean to, I can take the hurt away again, too."

He dropped his gaze to his hands, turning them palm up and back down again.

"Of course, I've never actually tried it out on purpose," he said with an ironic twist to his mouth.

Cat snorted.

"I should hope not! And in case you're wondering, I'm not volunteering to be your guinea pig, either."

"My what kind of pig?"

"Guinea pig."

He looked puzzled.

"What would I want with a pig?"

147

"Oh, that's just a phrase we have in my world. It's not about real pigs, I mean, pig-pigs. Guinea pigs are different, maybe you don't have them here."

"What are they?"

"They're small, furry animals, kind of like rabbits—do you have those?—without the long ears, and with a shorter head, and a more squat body, and shorter legs, and—"

"—and entirely un-rabbit-like on the whole?" he finished with a lopsided grin.

Cat just caught herself before she swatted him. Good heavens, apparently Yldra's behaviour was catching.

"You didn't let me finish! They're small, like rabbits, and furry, *like rabbits*, and children keep them as pets, *also like rabbits*. And of course they're both rodents."

"They sound like hedge-pigs, except soft and furry. And rodents."

"Oh, yes, and in all other ways entirely un-hedge-pig-like!" Cat scoffed, and Guy laughed. "What are hedge-pigs?" she asked, pleased with having scored one over him.

"They're small, too, about this big," he held his hands some six inches apart, "and prickly. And live in hedges. Haven't you ever seen one?"

"Oh, hedgehogs! No, actually, I've only seen pictures."

The kettle over the fire, which had been making quiet hissing noises for a while, had now progressed to enthusiastic bubbling, and steam rose from its spout.

Guy took the poker and used the hook on its end to swing the fireplace crane back outwards. He threw in a handful of dull green dry leaves from a round jar into a teapot he had waiting on the hearth, and filled it with boiling water. Sharp, fragrantly minty steam rose into the air.

"Mmm, that smells good." Cat reached for the cloth bundle Yldra had left on the table and unwrapped it. It held a lovely crusty brown loaf of bread and a chunk of solid yellow cheese.

"Do you have a knife?" she asked. "Or do you just break it up with your hands?"

Guy had both hands full, carrying the teapot in one and in the other a bouquet of three mugs held by the handles. "Over there," he said, pointing with his chin towards the fireplace, "in the cupboard."

"Over... where?" Cat stood in front of the shelves, scratching her head. What cupboard?

Guy stepped up behind her and reached over her shoulder. "Here," he said, opening a small door set into the wall beside the fireplace. Cat hadn't even seen the door handle, it blended so well with the wooden wall. This place seemed to be full of these secret storage places; it wasn't nearly as basic, let alone primitive, as Cat thought the first night she was there.

The cupboard held a basket full of carved wooden spoons and forks, and two or three vicious-looking metal knives with bone handles.

"This is the bread knife," Guy said, taking out one with a serrated blade. "I like using it for cheese too."

"Me too!" Cat said. "I mean, use bread knives for slicing cheese. Works better than straight ones for some reason."

Bibby got a mug of milk from the pitcher on the shelf with her bread and cheese, and the two adults enjoyed their tea. (Mintbrew, Cat mentally corrected herself. Mintbrew, and hedge pig, and wisewoman. And—and marriage chain. She was beginning to speak the language of this place.)

"So," Guy began around a mouthful of the chewy bread, "this place you came from, where there's no hedge pigs, but gunny pigs—"

"Guinea pigs."

"Yes, that. There was one of the bowls, and you just *looked* at it, and here you were?"

"That's about the size of it."

"Where exactly, here?"

"I told you, in the forest. A ways that-a-way." Cat waved her crumbly piece of yellow cheese in the general direction of the workshop. "You were passed out on the ground by this hole—" She shuddered. "That was scary, you know! I thought you were dead. And I don't *do* dead! Anyway, it was a muck hole—your clay pit, I suppose. How come you and Bibby were all clay-covered, anyway? Did you go bathing in the stuff? I didn't even recognize her as human at first; I thought she was some kind of alien."

Guy looked at her with a bemused expression. Did he even understand half of what she was talking about? For example, he probably didn't know what she meant by "alien". She shrugged.

"Like I said, I was pretty freaked out right then. And thankfully you weren't dead, so it's all good."

He had a wry twist to his mouth. "I prefer it that way, myself. But as to why we both were so dirty..." He frowned, trying to remember. "I went to fetch more clay, I know that. When we got to the clay pit—I was filling the bucket... And then Bibby fell in! That's right, the pit is getting low, she slipped down the edge, and all of a sudden she was right in it where it's most wet, face down. You can drown in that stuff—"

"Yes. You said, earlier." Quite dramatically, too.

"I—oh." He looked embarrassed.

Cat took pity on him. "So Bibby fell in and you pulled her out?"

"Yes, I had to get right into the pit myself. I got her out of the clay, and —I must have lost my footing, in a sink hole or something? I still had her in my arms, so I couldn't catch myself, and went down on my knee, and something under the surface jabbed me. Hard." He rubbed at his leg.

"Ow," said Cat sympathetically. "What about Bibby?"

"I... don't know... I don't remember anything after that..."

"So you didn't hit your head or anything?"

He shook his head. "I don't know... Was I in the pit when you found me?"

"No, you were lying across the path. Your leg was twisted, and you were covered in clay from head to toe. Thank goodness Ouska came running. She says she felt something, she knew there was something wrong with Bibby—but apparently it also had something to do with me touching a tree when I first arrived. I got an electric shock from it."

He looked at her intently.

"A tree? Where exactly was it? Right by the pit?"

"No, further down the path, around the corner. No idea what kind of tree it is, I've never seen one like it before. There are oaks around there, I recognized those, and evergreens. But this one is kind of smooth, and straight—and sticky; I got pitch on my fingers. There are some really gnarly trees around it, they make a sort of hedge, or screen or something..."

"The Arbour," he said quietly. "I might have known."

"And what's the Arbour when it's at home?" Cat was getting a little tired of all the mysterious references.

Guy crumbled a piece of cheese under his fingers.

"It's a place that's always been special to us, Sepp and me. I think it was Father who first took us there, when we were really young; I don't even remember. There is a tree there that's unusual, different from any others. A different colour, for one."

"Yes, it was kind of blue-ish!"

He nodded. "That screen you talked of, it goes all the way around it, shielding the tree—or maybe it's shielding everything else *from* the tree, I don't know. It well might be."

"Why, what's wrong with the tree?" Cat topped up her mug from the teapot.

"Nothing—or, perhaps, everything."

That wasn't cryptic at all. Cat raised her eyebrows quizzically.

"When I said I didn't know what made the glaze on those bowls turn out the way it did, that wasn't entirely true." Guy stared into the mug he held cupped between his hands. "I know what I did differently from my other glazes, but I don't know why it looks the way it does, or why the bowls—well, do what they do."

"And what you did differently was...?"

"There is ash from a big branch of that tree in that glaze. It was torn down, oh, years ago now, in a storm. I put it aside and then one day rendered it down into ash, and that's what made that glaze. That, and the clay from one particular part of the clay pit—as a matter of fact, I think it came right from where that sink hole is that made me fall."

"Huh, interesting. So the bowls are connected to that Arbour place, you think?"

He nodded, still frowning. "After—after what happened to Ashya, I didn't want to set foot in the Arbour ever again. And twice as much after Sepp. I know that tree has something to do with what happened. And that you—that this is where you first came here, and that it was one of those bowls that seems to have brought you, that proves it, doesn't it?"

CHAPTER 18

B IBBY SLURPED THE LAST bit of milk out of the bottom of her mug, then she gave a giant yawn, showing all her tiny pearly teeth.

"Goodness, someone's sleepy!" said Cat. She gave a questioning look at Guy. "Does she usually go to bed this early? It's not even dark yet."

"She's had a busy day playing with her cousins, so she's tired."

"All right then, munchkin," said Cat. "We'll deal with your milk moustache, and then it's pumpkin time."

She found a damp cloth and carried out this program, then while Guy cleared the table, she changed the little girl into her nightshirt.

"Come, let's have a cuddle," Cat said. She grabbed the blanket from the rocking chair, wrapped the baby in it, and sat down with her. (That rocking chair really was something else. Guy's brother was an amazing carpenter. Cat wished she could have met him and told him so.)

Bibby fussed and grizzled, rubbing her eyes.

"Oh shoosh," soothed Cat. "How about this?" She started singing.

"Twinkle, twinkle, little star," she sang, twinkling her fingers in front of the baby's face and gently rocking the chair in time to the tune, "how I wonder what you are, up above the world so high…"

Guy turned his head and looked at her with his eyebrows raised in surprise, and the tune dried up in Cat's throat. Ryan said she sounded like a crow, and he thought her library storytime songs were silly. (Ryan? Why had she ever put up with that self-absorbed idiot?)

"Sorry. I'll stop."

Guy shook his head. "No, no, don't stop. You have a nice voice. And see, the babe likes it."

Cat looked down to see the little girl sleepily wiggling her fingers, softly singing "Winka, winka…"

She smiled. What a darling. How could anyone not love her?

"Twinkle, twinkle, little star," she began again, "how I wonder what you are…"

She rocked, and sang, and Bibby's little head leaned against her, the eyelids drooping lower and lower. *One more song*, Cat thought, *and she'll be asleep.*

Cat leaned back against the headrest of the chair, closed her eyes, and softly sang:

"*Sleep, my child, and peace attend thee, all through the night;*

Guardian angels God will lend thee, all through the night;

Soft the drowsy hours are creeping, hill and dale in slumber steeping;

Love alone its watch is keeping, all through the night.

While the moon her watch is keeping, all through the night;

While the weary world is sleeping, all through the night;

O'er thy spirit gently stealing, visions of delight revealing,

Breathes a pure and holy feeling all through the night..."

She hummed the last few lines again, letting the final notes drop off into the silence.

The silence.

Cat suddenly became aware of the complete stillness in the room, all sound suspended in tension.

She opened her eyes to find Guy staring at her, his face pale, the turquoise eyes wide in shock.

He swallowed convulsively, as if he were trying to find his voice.

"That song!" he said finally, in a hoarse whisper. "You sang it, that night! It was no dream!"

Cat stared back at him, her eyes widening in response as she took in what he said.

He had been conscious. *Oh my God.*

"Did I..." he said, "you sang—Bibby had woken—"

Cat nodded, almost involuntarily.

"You were sick, delirious! You didn't know what you were saying!"

"But I did say it. I remember." Guy's voice sounded as if something was choking him; his eyes stood out hard against the unabated whiteness of his face. "And you—you answered.

"Didn't you?" he suddenly demanded harshly. "I asked you to marry me, and you said yes!"

Cat felt her face burning in a fiery blush.

"You didn't know what you were saying!" she repeated, almost pleadingly. "I had to humour you!"

He abruptly turned his head away, raising his clenched fist to his pressed-together lips.

Suddenly he turned on his heel, snatched a cloak from the hook on the back of the door, wrenched the door open, and limped out with long strides. Cat jumped as the door slammed shut.

"Guy, wait!"

Bibby stirred in Cat's arms, but she didn't wake.

Now what? Again with the histrionics!

Cat levered herself and the baby out of the rocking chair. Where could she put Bibby down? What would be a safe place for the little girl while she herself went after—

No. She couldn't leave the baby, it wasn't safe. All too well she remembered Guy's anger, and her own shock, at his wife's doing so, even if she herself had a much better reason. She'd have to take Bibby with her.

Very well. Needs must, as Uncle said. Cat wrapped the blanket more firmly around the little girl, jiggled her up in her arms to get a firm grip on her, and stepped out into the gathering dusk.

"Guy!"

Which way had he gone?

And there it was. An unmistakable, solid, clear direction: he had gone into the Wald.

Catriona knew it as surely as if she could see and hear him limping ahead in front of her. He was going to the Arbour, that special place which belonged to him and his brother, which was connected with the disappearance of his wife, where Cat herself had arrived in this country.

There was just enough light to see the way, the path by which Cat and Ouska had carried the wounded man to the cottage—was it really only two days ago?

Bibby, sleeping soundly, was heavy in Cat's arm, and the blanket kept slipping. *Hurry, Cat...* There was the clay pit—she gave it a wide berth; she had conceived a great respect for that big mud hole.

The buckets still lay in the path. Or rather, one of them did, the other had rolled into the pit and was half sunk into the clay by now.

We'll have to come back and collect them tomorrow, Cat thought, *Guy needs them.* Then she caught herself up, startled. What was with the "we"? It was as if she expected to be here tomorrow and the day after that and the day after that, as if—as if this was where she belonged. As if, two days ago, she's hadn't been an ordinary person, ex-librarian, ex-girlfriend of a stuck-up guy named Ryan; ordinary, boring, intimidated by the thought of booking a plane ticket to a tame city just because she'd never been there before.

Hurry! the voice in her head commanded.

Cat hurried.

She felt every root and rock through the soft leather of her moccasins—*Don't stub your toe, Cat*—and once again hitched the baby higher in her arms. There was the bend in the path beyond the clay pit.

Cat broke into a stumbling run—*Don't trip, Cat*—the sleeping little girl bouncing in her arms.

"Guy!" she called, "Guy!" Where was the man?

She just heard the noise over the sound of her own steps and breathing—crashing, cracking, breaking branches—and then she stood in the archway to that little clearing, the Arbour.

She had found Guy.

With furious energy, he was ripping and tearing at the overhanging branches of the blue tree.

CHAPTER 19

"**G**UY! STOP! WHAT ARE you doing?"

With a few steps, Cat was beside him, and she reached out a hand to grab at his arm.

He whirled around at her touch, his eyes blazing turquoise.

But his bad leg gave out at the sudden motion; he cried out, staggered, swayed, and clutched at his knee, barely catching himself from falling. He stood like this, half-crouched, his head bowed, drawing a deep breath, then another, and another, and finally breathed out a deep sigh.

When he looked up, the fury had drained from his eyes. Slowly he straightened, steadying himself on the branches he had been tearing at just a minute ago.

"You're here," he said, bewildered. "You came. Why did you come?"

Oh, for heaven's sakes, enough with the dramatics! Cat's adrenaline rush was ebbing, leaving her not a little exasperated.

"Of course I came," she said briskly, looking around for a suitable spot to sit. "You give me dramatic looks, then you storm out of the house, leaving me holding the baby. Who, incidentally, is getting really heavy." She spotted a large flattish rock, brushed it off with her foot, and sat down on it, settling Bibby on her lap. "What was I meant to do, sit there and wait until you come back? *If* you come back? I've had about enough. So suppose you tell me what's going on?"

His eyes never wavered from her face as he painfully limped over and settled himself on the ground beside her.

(*He's hurt his knee again with his carelessness. Figures,* thought Cat. *I'll have to get Ouska to give me more ointment for it.* And once more she pulled herself up short—there was that assumption again that it was her task to look after him, that she would be there to do it...)

"Well?" Cat gave Guy a straight look, the determined one that was most effective with library patrons who tried to wiggle out of their overdue fines.

Guy looked down at his feet and pulled out a small stick from under his right heel. He cleared his throat.

"It's true, isn't it," he stated, breaking inch-long pieces off the stick and dropping them between his feet. "I asked you to marry me, and you said yes." A fourth piece followed the first three.

"Yes," said Cat, and wondered that she wasn't blushing this time. "Yes, it's true, not yes, I'll marry you. Like I said, I'm quite sure you didn't know what you were saying. I certainly didn't think you did; you even called me by some other name, I can't remember what it was..." (*That was a lie, Cat. You know exactly what he called you. And you know there's something important about it.*)

"It doesn't matter," he said dully. "I *was* conscious, and I remember what I said. How I said it. And what you answered. Don't you see—" (the last piece of stick was snapped in half) "—those were the words of marriage."

"What?!? What on earth do you mean?"

He looked up at her, his brows drawn together in pain.

"It does not mean we *will* marry, it means we already *are.*"

Okay, Cat, don't hyperventilate.

"It can't! I didn't mean what I said!"

"I know. But that doesn't matter. You said it, and that makes it true. Damn!" He slammed his fist into the little pile of stick pieces between his feet.

Not very flattering, a voice in the corner of Cat's mind said. *Is it so upsetting to marry me? But then, I guess men don't want me. Just look at Ryan.*

Aloud she said, "I don't understand. Just because we said those words—that makes us married? What about—what about some kind of ceremony? That chain thing? Can't we just un-say the words?"

"I don't think so." He had found another stick and was mangling it. "The wedding chain, it's the second part of it. The words are the first. But they're just as binding." He fell silent.

Cat stared at the tree trunks across from them, not really seeing them, even though the light was still just bright enough to make out the individual branches.

So what did this mean then? Was there no way out? They *were* in the place where she had first arrived. Maybe that magical tree he had mentioned...

"Guy, what were you doing, ripping at those branches there?"

He looked up at the tree screen.

"I—I hardly know. This is damnable, all of it. I thought, somehow, it's that tree that's at the root of it all, it started with the tree... I know the real fault is mine, but I thought—no, I didn't really think. I was just angry. I've trapped you, just like I trapped *her*. It can't happen again, not again—I need to find a way out... and the tree, perhaps..."

Suddenly, the air in front of them began to shimmer. An iridescent glow, sparkling and shining in the dusk, became a whirling vortex, like a miniature tornado.

The luminescence thinned, then dissolved, revealing at its centre a person with his back to them.

He staggered, lost his balance, and fell backwards, landing hard on his rear end.

Cat stared.

He wore a light-coloured, snug-fitting t-shirt and a dark pair of jeans, a pair of sneakers on his feet. His black hair was long enough to brush the collar of his shirt, and he clutched something in his hands, something that looked like a bowl.

He swivelled his head, staring at the trees around him, then turned right around, looking behind him, and his eyes met Cat's.

They spoke at the same time.

163

"It's *you!*"

It was the turquoise-eyed man from the Sammelhauser Museum.

CHAPTER 20

G UY MADE A STRANGLED noise and started to his feet. He stared at the newcomer as if he were seeing a ghost, his face ghastly white in the gloom of the dusk.

Then several things happened at once.

"Guy!" cried the man, and his face broke into an enormous, lopsided grin. He sprang forward, dropping the bowl; Guy practically leapt towards him, and the two collided, throwing their arms around each other in a tremendous hug.

But the sudden movement was too much for Guy's leg; he gave a yelp of pain and lost his balance, pulling the other man with him, who stepped on the bowl on the ground, cracking it in two.

With all the commotion, Bibby was startled awake and began to cry.

"Shoosh, shoosh!" Cat soothed.

The newcomer, laughing, helped Guy to regain his balance, then he peered at the little girl. Once again he broke into his brilliant smile.

"Bibby Karana! It's you!"

That name again!

Bibby stopped crying, her mouth open, and stared up at him, then she smiled her sweet baby smile.

"Uncayepp!" she said, turning up her face to Cat's to see how she felt about this.

Cat looked from one pair of brilliantly turquoise eyes to the other, then to Guy, who stood clutching his knee, but nonetheless smiling as broadly (and lopsidedly) as the other man. The only thing she had left to wonder was why she hadn't made the connection before. How many pairs of turquoise eyes could there be in the world—even a foreign, magical one?

She felt an answering smile spreading over her face.

"The Septimissimus, I presume?" she said.

The newcomer, whose resemblance to Guy ended with his smile and eye colour, gave her a bow. He was easily half a head shorter than his brother, his hair nearly black, and his build solid rather than slender. Cat thought there was room for excuses here—the two hardly looked like brothers, definitely not at first glance.

"And you are Cat," he said.

Then he turned to Guy, with a look of urgency on his face.

"Guy! Guy, she's there!"

"What? Who? Where?" Guy seemed as confused as Cat was.

"She's there!" Guy's brother repeated. "The place I just came from, where *she's* from," he gestured at Cat, "Ashya is there!" He grabbed Guy by the shoulders. "She's not dead, Guy! She's alive!"

Confusion, hope, and something undefinable chased each other over Guy's face.

"You've seen her?"

"Seen her, spoken with her, and, uh, stolen..." He let go of Guy and looked around on the ground. "...stolen this from her," he finished, poking with his foot at the two uneven pieces the bowl had cracked into. He leaned down to peer at them in the dark. "Hmm, just like the other one," he said.

"What other one?" Cat got up from her rock.

"The one that brought you here," Sepp said. "Here, do you want me to take the babe?" He reached out his arms for Bibby.

The little girl shook her head and snuggled deeper into Cat's arms, reaching up around Cat's neck and holding on. Cat had to make an effort to not let her face show how smug she felt at this. She wrapped her arms tighter around the warm little body and hugged her close.

"Hoh," said Sepp, "what's this then?" He gave a quizzical look at his brother, who still stood hunched over, rubbing his injured leg with a grimace of pain. Sepp's eyebrow rose. "And what have you done to yourself this time?"

"Slipped in the clay pit," Guy replied briefly. "Let's go home. We can talk about it there."

—ele—

It was a slow progress getting back to the cottage. Guy was so sore he needed his brother to support him for most of

167

the way, and Cat herself was glad for the short breaks they took so he could rest—Bibby got heavier the farther she had to carry her. The slump of the little girl's head on her shoulder told her she had dropped off to sleep again.

By the time they finally reached the cottage, it was almost completely dark. The fire in the hearth was still burning gently, the logs nearly spent.

With a relieved groan, Guy sank into the chair by the table and propped his left foot up on the bench.

"Feed the fire, young 'un," he commanded, "and light us a light!"

"I hear and obey, oh ancient one!" mocked his brother, the words clearly an old ritual between them. He put the pot shards he had been carrying on the table, then took a log from the stack beside the fireplace and dropped it on top of the embers in the hearth. "Got any spills?"

"Jar, by the lights," Guy replied, gesturing at the pottery cup on the mantelpiece filled with what Cat had thought were wooden skewers.

Sepp took one of the skinny sticks, lit its end in the fire, and brought the flame up to the candles above the hearth. He carried one of the candles over to the table. The brown teapot still stood there, and he lifted it up and swirled it to test for contents.

"Any mintbrew left?"

"I don't think so," Guy said. "Make some more?"

"Oh yes, please," said Cat, who was tucking the sleeping baby into Guy's bed. She rubbed her arms and gave a shiver. "I could use some hot t—mintbrew."

"Tea, you call it, don't you?" Sepp asked. "Or that's what Nicky says."

Cat's head shot up.

"You've met Nicky?!?"

"*Oh* yes!" Sepp replied feelingly. "Met her, spent the night in her rooms, got these from her..." He gestured at what he was wearing. A white Nike T-shirt, black button-fly jeans, high-top sneakers with loose laces.

"Ah, I thought I'd seen that outfit before! Didn't that belong to—" She clapped her hand over her mouth. *Very tactful, Cat.*

"Uh, yes. I understand it belonged to a previous 'boy friend' who left it behind when he moved out."

Guy's eyebrows were vying for space with his hairline as he looked from one of them to the other.

Sepp grinned at him. "They have rather different ways of doing things in that place," he said.

Cat slid onto the back bench between the table and wall, planted her elbows on the bare wood surface, put her chin on her fists, and gave Sepp a stern look.

"So, talk!" she commanded. "And start at the beginning. I'm tired of people throwing random bits of information at me that make no sense."

The brothers exchanged a glance, and Guy's mouth twitched up at the corner just a little.

"You'd better do as she says," he recommended.

Sepp finished with the kettle by the fire, and now came over to the table with the filled teapot and some mugs.

"What's the beginning?" he asked, straddling the front bench next to Guy's propped-up foot. "When I met you? When I left here?"

He poured the tea into the mugs and pushed one across the table to Cat. It bumped into the pot shards lying between them, which the light of the candle showed to be a dull, rusty brown. Sepp picked up one of the pieces and fingered it thoughtfully.

"I suppose the beginning is those bowls," he said. He looked at Guy. "Have you found out what does it?"

Guy shook his head, his lips pressed together.

"Well, it's a strange thing," Sepp said. "When you touch one, everything goes into a swirl, sort of spinning around you in circles."

"Yes!" cried Cat. "That's just what happened to me!"

"But you said you didn't touch it, didn't you?" said Guy.

"Well, now that I think of it, I guess my hair brushed against it when I bent over it to look at it. But you actually had it in your hands, Sepp, right?"

"Yes, and I still did when I landed on the other side. Everything whirls around you, and when it settles and stops spinning, you're someplace else. And every time I land on my backside." He laughed and rubbed his tailbone.

Cat chuckled. "Precisely. So where did you end up landing?"

"I came out in this grassy little area behind that large building. The musean, I think?"

"Museum," Cat corrected. "So you've been around the Sammelhauser Museum the whole time?"

"Yes—well, no—yes, until I saw you, and then you disappeared again, and—"

"Stop! One thing at a time. So you landed behind the museum, with the bowl still in your hand. This bowl?" Cat pointed to the broken shards on the table.

"No. The one that you looked at. This one is the one that—oh, all right, one step at a time!" He grinned at Cat's stern look. "But you keep interrupting!"

Cat quirked up the corner of her mouth. He had a point.

"Okay, I'll shut up. You tell your story. You landed behind the museum..."

"Yes. It's enormous, Guy! And there's other buildings even bigger, they go way higher than two floors there! Uncle Ardross would love to get a look at that."

Cat opened her mouth to comment, then shut it again with an audible snap. Sepp looked at her and winked.

"As I was saying," he continued, "there was this enormous building in front of me. But other than that, once my head stopped spinning, I thought I'd just landed someplace else in Isachang—Ilim, maybe, or even the capital. You see, just around the corner, there was a market, just like ours here. Or I thought it was, at first. Most people were dressed normally, like this," he gestured at the clothes Cat and Guy were wearing, "although some were in really bright colours and odd styles. But I thought that was just city fashions.

"They had a hand-to-hand fighting arena, like the ones we heard about in stories, Guy, and stalls where they sold

171

things; just like an ordinary market. Food, clothes, leather goods, even a potter.

"I wandered around, trying to determine just what had happened to me and where I was, so I started talking to the stallholders. Several of them commented on my clothes, and one said I was 'really in character'—she seemed to think that was a good thing..."

Cat had listened to all this with a puzzled frown, but now the penny dropped.

"The Renaissance Fair!" she said. "I forgot they had that there last weekend! Is that where you met Nicky?"

Sepp gave her a mock frown.

"Oops, sorry," Cat said, "shutting up again."

He grinned. "Well, as you say, the Whatever-you-call-it Fair. Nicky seems quite excited about those. No, that's not where I met her. And yes, before you ask, I still had the bowl. Not this bowl, the other bowl. And no, it didn't look like this, it still looked different. And no—"

"Cut it out!" Cat said, punching him in the arm.

Since when had she started acting like that? Almost as if they were her brothers. She'd never had brothers. Brothers? Did Guy feel like a brother? Cat's mind skittered away from that line of thinking.

"Okay, so, Ren Fair. What happened?"

"Not much else. I met some people around that jousting arena who seemed to think I belonged to another part of their group, another chapter, they called it. They shared their food and even let me sleep in their tent. At that point I still thought it was all a wonderful adventure, and I was only too glad to be away from here." He looked a silent apology at his brother. "By the next day it had begun to dawn on me that I'd landed myself in a place that was... very different from here."

"No kidding," Cat said quietly. It was hard enough going from the modern world to here, but the other way around? She couldn't even imagine.

Sepp exchanged a look with her. "Yes, well. By then I was wondering very much what actually had happened to me, if I wasn't in some kind of fever dream or—or had gone insane. I'm quite sure I wasn't the only one wondering that, by some of the looks I got. I did ask a lot of questions that must have sounded very strange... And then there was the way I was clutching that bowl and trying all sorts of weird things with it."

He gave a snort.

"There is one girl that will probably never get over seeing me wear it on my head for half an hour straight, like a hat. Other than terrifying her into thinking me a lunatic, it didn't do anything. Nothing whatsoever. And neither did any of the other things I tried to do with it, I'll spare you the details.

"It hadn't changed then, looked just like it had when I picked it up here, with that bright blue-green glaze. I didn't see why it couldn't take me back the way I had come. Still don't see it, in fact; I don't understand..." His voice trailed off and he stared into the candle flame.

"But you did come back," Cat prompted gently.

Sepp looked up.

"Not for a long while. It seemed—it seemed forever, at least until..."

"One thing at a time?" suggested Cat with a smile.

He smiled back. "All right. One thing at a time. So that Fair broke up, which, to be honest, was rather a relief. I'd realized by then they were all just playacting, and it confused me more than anything. But I still had no way to get home.

"One of the fairgoers who'd stayed behind let me sleep the night in his caravan—Guy, those caravans, their carriages! You wouldn't *believe* it! They're—" He broke off. "Never mind."

"So then what?"

"I hadn't given up hope of finding a way to get home. I was still hanging around the musean—museum—trying to decide what to do next.

"And then I saw *you*." He looked at Cat. "You got out of that enormous closed carriage (the bus, Nicky calls it?), and suddenly I knew you'd be my way back. Are you an Unissima, by chance?"

That again!

"I don't—people keep saying that. So, well, maybe." Cat thought of how she had known where to find Guy in the forest. "What does that have to do with it?"

"If you are, it would explain why I knew it was you. You know, Guy, how Aunt's Knowing sometimes spills over onto the people she is with?" Guy nodded. "It was like that," Sepp said. "I just knew."

"You freaked me right out, staring at me like that," Cat said, "and stalking me!"

"I'm sorry," Sepp said, and he actually sounded like he meant it. "I didn't know what else to do. I had to get you to

174

the bowl, make you look at it. Well, I thought you'd have to pick it up, but it turns out you didn't need to after all. I put it in that glass case, with the ugly frog, and then I—sorry, I stalked you."

He huffed out a laugh.

"It actually took you quite a long time to notice me, inside the museum. There were several rooms where you wouldn't even look up, you were so fascinated with the things in the glass boxes."

"Oy!" Cat said. "You mean you, you..."

Sepp shrugged and grinned.

"You finally saw me, and moved into the room with the bowl. I didn't want to follow you so closely that you'd get frightened into running away altogether, so I held back, and I almost missed it."

"Missed what?"

"I came around the corner, and just saw you bending down to look at the bowl, then closer—and then you were gone. Just like that."

Guy made an inarticulate noise.

Sepp gave him a questioning look.

"Go on," Cat said quietly. "I was gone..."

"I ran over to where you'd been. But there was no sign of you anywhere. Nothing. And when I looked at the bowl, it looked like this." He gestured at the shards on the table. "See how it's gone that rusty brown? The same."

"Huh, interesting."

"Yes. I looked all around the room for you—remember, I was certain that you were my way home. But you were gone. The only sign that was left of you was your satchel."

"My satchel? Oh, you mean my purse? You found my purse?"

"I picked it up, and I thought that, I don't know, maybe that I'd mistaken what I saw, and you'd actually run away after all. Suddenly I was sure you'd left the museum, so I ran after you.

"And just when I got out through the main doors, your bag started singing."

CHAPTER 21

"MY BAG WAS SINGING?!?" cried Cat.

Guy gave his brother a strange look. "And just what were you drinking?"

"It's true! The bag was singing! Some very odd-sounding song about not worrying and being happy; there were even instruments playing with it."

Cat threw back her head and laughed.

"My cell phone! That's too funny! That song is the dial tone, Nicky put it on there for a joke."

"I didn't know that, did I? So at first I thought you'd shrunk down to really tiny and had crawled inside your satchel, singing from inside it." Sepp looked from Cat to his brother's skeptical face. "What? I'd just been kidnapped by a bowl and transported to another world! Anything could be possible!"

"Fair enough," Cat said, thinking of her theories about aliens and giant insect cultures.

"So then I tried to open the bag to get you out, but it was fused shut at the top. Clasped together with very small teeth. And all the time it kept singing at me!

"And all of a sudden somebody tore it out of my hands, and then hit me with it and screamed at me, calling me a thief and a scumbag and who knows what else." Sepp rubbed his shoulder and gave Cat a reproachful look. "You have some very hard-edged things in that satchel. And your friend is violent. Not to mention, um, creative with her language."

"Nicky? Oh my goodness. I was supposed to meet her at the museum. She probably tried to call my cell when she got there and I wasn't outside waiting for her. That's why my phone would have been ringing; nobody else ever calls me on that."

"Whatever you say. So finally she let up hitting me with your satchel, but then she yelled that she had a mace, and she would use it if I tried anything, but all I could see was a little metal tube she was pointing at me, with her finger right on top—"

Cat clapped her hand over her mouth.

"Oh no! She didn't!"

"Didn't what?"

"Pepper-spray you!"

"Is that what that was? No, no pepper, fortunately; it makes me sneeze."

"Uh, that's not quite... But, thank goodness for small mercies. Then what?"

"Well, she'd stopped hitting me, but she wasn't done yelling. She kept saying what had I done with Cat, and if you were hurt she'd have my guts for garters, and where were you, and on and on. So I told her."

"And she believed you??"

"Yes—well, no—well, eventually. At least she stopped screeching. And then a large man came out of the musean—"

"Museum."

"Yes, that. I think he was some kind of watchman. He asked if there was a problem, but I guess by then she'd decided I was harmless—"

Guy gave a snort, and Sepp looked at him indignantly.

"I said 'harmless,' not 'gormless.' She told the man she could handle the situation, and he went away again. And then she dragged me inside, and we went through the whole place three times over to make sure you really, really, *really* weren't anywhere in that building. By then, Nicky had seen that I was nearly as frantic about finding you as she was. So she took me home with her, to her rooms. Oh stars, the way we got there..." He made a face.

Cat chuckled. "Nicky's a bit of an, uh, adventuresome driver."

Sepp huffed air out between his lips.

"If *you* even say that, and you're used to those vehicles..."

Guy looked from one of them to the other, puzzled.

"Their carriages drive *on their own*, Guy!" Sepp said. "No horses, no nothing! Just roaring noises and stinking smoke, and they go at speeds you can't even imagine!"

Guy's eyebrows were climbing his forehead again.

"It's true!" Sepp insisted.

Cat nodded. "It is. They work on an internal combustion engine."

Now Guy looked puzzled as well as incredulous.

"Never mind," Cat said. "So you went home with Nicky, and then what?"

She felt a blush spread over her face as she realized what she'd just said, but thankfully the men seemed oblivious to it.

"She let me sleep on her sofa, and the next day we went out looking for you. Or rather, she looked and I came along. She made me put on these clothes as she said it would make me less noticeable."

"Well, yes, they would. It was your outfit that was the first thing I noticed about you."

Sepp shrugged. "We kept looking, and of course found no sign of you. But this morning..." He gave Cat a sidelong glance, then reached for the teapot and poured himself another cup of mintbrew.

What wasn't he saying about the time in between? He and Nicky had hardly spent every second of the time he was there combing the town for Cat.

"This morning..." she prompted, taking another sip from her own mug.

"This morning," he continued, "Nicky suddenly thought of this friend of yours, that Ryan."

Cat choked.

"Ryan?" she managed when she finished coughing. "Whatever made Nicky think of him?"

"I'm not sure—but I'm glad she did. Because," Sepp turned to Guy, "that's where we met Ashya."

"*What*?!?"

Sepp still looked at his brother.

"She's changed, Guy. She's not the same woman—but yet, she is. It's hard to explain." He scratched the corner of his jaw. "It's like she's more herself than she ever was here. She seems to *belong* there. You know how she used to wear her hair all piled on the top of her head? Now it's all down her back, and it's even fairer than it was, with all these pale and golden streaks in it, and all, oh—" He waved his hands about, drawing curlicues in the air. "It's strange, but it suits her. As for her clothes—oh my." His eyes widened at the mental image. "Is that normal, Cat? I didn't see a lot of other women dressing that way. Nicky doesn't, nor you."

"What way?" Cat asked, even though she had a pretty good idea of what he was getting it.

"You know how most women wear trousers there—I mean, that seems practical. But Ashya, she had on something that might have been a skirt once, before someone took off the bottom part and left only the top band."

Cat nearly snorted her tea out through her nose. That was the best description of a miniskirt she'd ever heard.

"She didn't have much of a shirt either, and what little there was was all sparkly and bright purple. And her shoes looked quite hard to balance on—the heels were tiny stilts, and they had some sort of fluff across the toes, also purple. I don't know why she even bothered with them inside. I thought at first she had come to the door in her underclothes, but then that man she was with, that Ryan, didn't seem to think anything of it."

"Ryan." Cat said the name in a carefully casual tone. "Nicky thought he might know where I was?"

"Yes. I'd told her over and over about the bowls, how you just vanished. She couldn't—well, I think she wanted to believe me, but couldn't make herself. Not quite. And you can't really blame her."

"No, you can't. But..."

"By then she'd exhausted all other ideas. We were getting desperate. So she thought, maybe this Ryan fellow had seen you, or perhaps he still had some things of yours you'd wanted to go back for, or something. She said he used to be your 'boy friend'—that means something like courting, doesn't it?"

Out of the corner of her eye, Cat could see Guy's astonished expression. She wanted to sink into the floor.

"Yes," she said, doodling on the tabletop with her finger dipped into the water ring that was left where her mug had dribbled a little. "Yes, he was my boyfriend. Operative word 'was.' He dumped me." She looked at Guy, willing him to understand.

"Dumped you?" the potter said with a frown.

"Broke up with me. Didn't want me. Decided he had enough of being with me. It wasn't really me he was interested in in the first place, just my position in the town—I worked at the library. Do you have those here? Places where you keep books for people to read? I haven't seen any books around here." She looked around the room as if she were hoping some novels had suddenly materialized on the mantelpiece.

"Certainly we've got books," said Sepp. "It's just Guy, he doesn't like them much."

Guy scowled at his brother.

"It's not that I don't like them," he explained to Cat, "they're just not much use for me. The letters never stand still long enough for me to read them. As Sepp knows full well."

Sepp grinned at him, then turned back to Cat.

"You were saying, this Ryan…"

Cat swallowed hard around the lump in her throat. Her gambit to distract them from her pathetic love life by a change of topic hadn't worked.

"I was just saying he was never interested in me, really, just in my position, in who he thought I was. I suppose if I was a bit brighter I'd have realized that from the start."

"Hmm, where have we heard that one before?" mused Sepp, staring up into the air over his head. "Someone feigning to be in love with a person because of their position, or their family—and of course, being good-looking helps, too…"

"Oh no, it wasn't that." Cat knew that for a fact. "It was just the job; he figured I was important. He never thought I was good-looking."

Sepp tilted his head and gave Cat a carefully considering look.

"This Ryan fellow didn't *look* blind," he said thoughtfully. "But with all the amazing things they can do in that world of yours, maybe they can make a stone-blind man look like he's in full possession of his sight? Sure could have fooled me." He looked at Guy. "It's the only explanation, wouldn't you say?"

The corner of Guy's mouth quirked up, but his tone was quite bland. "Not the only one. Blithering idiocy could be the other."

"Oh, yes, quite!" agreed Sepp eagerly, leaning forward on his elbows as if he were ready to settle in for a discussion of the visual or mental faculties of Ryan the Ex for the rest of the night. "I did see some signs..."

"Stop it!" Cat said, her face flaming. "Both of you!"

The men chuckled. A warm feeling spread through Cat's body, and a sidelong glance at Guy showed that he was regarding her with a lopsided smile.

"So, this Ashya," she said quickly—maybe this time they'd take the bait and change the subject—"what was she doing at Ryan's place?"

"Apparently she is his new 'girl friend.' Or so he told Nicky, when she asked about you. He had a new girl friend, he said, someone who suited him better. And he drew this woman forward by the hand with a smarmy smirk, and it was Ashya. Except he called her Ashley."

Something clicked in Cat's head. Ashley? Long, curled, blonde hair, tight clothes, stiletto-heeled purple mules? A picture rose to the surface.

"Ashley?" she cried. "Ashley the Model? *That's* Ashya?"

"You know her?" asked Sepp.

"I know *of* her. Ashley the Model—oh dear me yes, what a perfect match for Ryan. They'd suit each other down to the ground. Nicky met her before, didn't she say?"

"There really was no opportunity. Nicky pushed her way through the door into the rooms—the apartment, she called it; I think she had some idea the Ryan fellow was hiding you there. He followed her, probably to stop her breaking things, the mood she was in." Sepp made a scoffing noise. "He should have kept an eye on me instead."

"What do you mean?"

"Ashya stood there, staring at me. She'd recognized me right away, quicker than I her (I did say she's changed). She had that pout on her face, you know the one, Guy."

Guy's nostrils pinched down as if he had caught a whiff of something unpleasant. Apparently he knew exactly what Sepp meant.

"She wasn't coming back, she said, oh no," Sepp continued. "That place was so amazing, and people appreciated her properly, and she had an agent and found her niche—whatever she meant by that—so I'd wasted my time coming after her. I didn't bother telling her that coming after her had been the last thing on my mind. But I thought that she could have pretended a little bit of interest in, well, if not in you, Guy, at least in Bibby, and I said so."

He looked at the sleeping baby on the bed, a scowl drawing down his brows.

"That made her sulk outright. She wasn't cut out to be a mother, she said, and the baby was cute, but she wasn't ever having another one. Fortunately, they had ways to make sure of that there."

"Oh!" said Cat. That would explain the thing about Bibby "coming into her powers" so early!

The men looked at her, but she shook her head. "Never mind, carry on. What happened with Ashya?"

185

"I was still standing at the door of the rooms," Sepp said. "All of a sudden I felt this pull, an irresistible yearning for home, as if something had called to me. And then I saw the bowl. Yes, this bowl." He poked the shards on the table. "But it was still bright, as blue as the others. It sat on a table in the first room, just beyond the door.

"Ashya saw me looking at it, and said that yes, that was what had brought her there, and she didn't know how it had done it, but it wasn't doing it anymore. She just kept it because it matched her colour scheme. Then she turned around and swanned out of the room.

"And I—I couldn't bear to leave one of your bowls with her, Guy, just because it matched the stripes in the wallpaper." He scoffed. "So I picked it up."

"And?" Cat leaned forward on her elbows.

"And the next thing I knew I was on my backside in the Wald! And I must say, Guy, I've never been so glad to see anyone in my life as you at that moment!"

He was speaking to his brother, but he looked at Cat as he said it, a gleam in his eye.

Cat smiled at him. She liked this man, a lot. Almost as much as... *Stop, Cat. Don't go there.*

Suddenly she saw a light passing by in the darkness of the forest outside the window.

"I think someone's coming," she said.

CHAPTER 22

A SHORT RAP SOUNDED on the door, followed immediately by the door being pushed open.

Ouska entered the room carrying a lantern. She gazed around the room, and when her eyes fell on Sepp, her whole face lit up.

But all she said, in a curt tone, was, "So you're back, are you?"

"Good evening, Aunt," the young man replied meekly, his eyes dancing in response to her unspoken pleasure at his return. He got to his feet. Guy followed suit, struggling to stand up.

"Sit," the older woman told the potter. "I'm just as well off on the bench."

Guy gratefully sank back into the chair, while Sepp moved around to the back of the table.

"Move over a bit, will you," he said to Cat, sliding onto the bench beside her. She obligingly scooted a foot sideways, closer to Guy, who had his foot up on the front bench again.

Ouska got a mug from the shelf, then settled herself at the table and poured a cup of mintbrew. She took a slow sip, letting her eyes travel over the three young faces across from her.

Cat sat up straighter. She almost felt as if she was being evaluated. There was something about the wise-woman that really made Cat want her approval. But not just that—she wanted her respect. She swallowed her self-consciousness and met Ouska's gaze with a steady one of her own.

The older woman's brown eyes locked with Cat's for a brief moment, then she gave her an infinitesimal nod, as if she were pleased with her. Cat secretly released a pent-up breath.

Ouska's gaze moved on to Sepp, and then down to the bowl shards on the table.

"So you're back," she repeated. "When? About an hour back, two?"

"Yes," Sepp and Cat replied at the same time, then they looked at each other and laughed.

"In the Wald," Cat continued. "The same place where I first landed."

"Yes, I felt it. And just exactly where was that again?" Ouska had an intent look in her eyes.

"There's a little clearing..."

"The Arbour," said Sepp. "They were there, waiting. Come to think of it, I have no idea why."

"Guy went there, and I followed him. It was something to do with a tree?" She looked at the potter, waiting for him to pick up the thread, but he remained silent, his expression shuttered.

"The tall one," Sepp said, "with the blue bark? Behind the screen?"

"The Septimus Tree," said Ouska matter-of-factly. It was clear that this was no surprise to her.

"What?" Sepp and Guy had spoken at the same time, and they stared at their aunt.

"Didn't you know its name? It was planted by your ancestor, the last Septimissimus, nearly seven hundred years ago. It's special to your family, and it has particular powers for the Septimus."

"So that's why Father took us there..." began Sepp.

Ouska nodded. "Yes, that's why. I've been suspecting that tree had much to do with what's been happening this last while."

"So you were right, Guy!" Cat said.

The potter stared at his aunt.

"Perhaps," the older woman said, "though I suspect that it's not quite the way you think."

"What do you mean?" Guy said, his voice rough.

Ouska laid a gentle hand on his lower leg, resting on the bench beside her. "You were far more ill that you should have been with an injury of this kind."

Cat nodded. His passing out, just from slipping in the mud, had never made much sense.

"But then, you recovered much faster than could be expected after such a grave illness. I believe it due to this." Ouska reached into a little pocket on the waistband of her skirt and brought out a small bundle wrapped in a handkerchief. She folded back the cloth and held the contents up to the light.

Cat recoiled. Held up in Ouska's hand, grasped in the handkerchief, was the sharp splinter she had removed from Guy's wound the morning before.

But then Cat leaned closer, intrigued. Even in the low, yellow light of the candle she could see what was unusual about this. This was no ordinary wood—it had a distinctly turquoise-blue sheen. She looked from Guy to Ouska and back again.

"That's the sliver that was stuck in your leg, Guy," Cat said slowly, putting the pieces together in her head as she spoke. "It was in the clay pit, in the very part of it where, you said, you'd taken the clay from to mix the glaze for the blue bowls. And that stick is blue, too—it's a piece of that tree, isn't it?"

She looked at Ouska for confirmation, who nodded at her to carry on.

"It was the ashes from that tree that made the other part of that glaze," Cat continued. "The splinter in your leg made you so horribly sick. The glaze on the bowls, which was made from that wood and the clay the wood had soaked in, makes people leave, or come back to this world just by that tree. My touching the tree alerted Ouska to my being here, and I think it was your touching it, trying to break off some branches, that drew Sepp back home."

She fell silent for a moment.

"But one thing I don't understand: why is it Guy's pottery, even if it does come from the Septimus tree, that has that special power, when it's Sepp who is the Septimissimus?"

At this, Ouska nodded again, like a teacher pleased with a favourite pupil who made all the right connections and correctly solved the most difficult exam question.

She drew back her shoulders.

"But he is not," she said. "Sepp is not the Septimissimus—Guy is."

CHAPTER 23

THE THREE YOUNG PEOPLE stared at the older woman, wide-eyed in surprise.

"I suspected it before," Ouska said, "but now I am certain."

Cat could tell it was not easy for her to continue.

"I had a sister," Ouska began.

A sister? What about that 'only daughter of an only daughter' thing?

The older woman saw Cat's unspoken question. "She was my half-sister, my father's daughter, not my mother's. My brother and sister were still small when my father married my mother, his second wife, and she raised them as her own. Nevertheless, I was the only daughter born of her body.

"We lost her when I was twenty-two. My sister missed her as much as I did, and if my mother had still been alive... My sister wanted guidance. We were both of us in love, though no one knew of hers. Uncle and I, we had just come to an understanding, and I was wrapped up in my own happiness."

She looked down at her hands, which lay folded together in her lap.

"It's the regret of my life that I did not listen to the Knowing that day, when it told me my sister was in trouble and needed my help. I felt it, but I was so new to the Knowing that I did not heed its urgency. I delayed, shrugged it off. When I finally went to her, it was too late.

"You see, she was with child. That, too, she had hid from the world, just as they had hid their love for one another, she and Salmor."

Guy's and Sepp's heads snapped back in an almost identical motion, and they stared at their aunt slack-jawed.

"Yes." The older woman nodded. "She carried your father's child. I know that now—but all these years, I was never certain if it really was his, if it was he who was her secret lover. That day, she miscarried. Lost the babe, and then we lost her." Ouska's voice was heavy with remembered sadness.

"But—but Father never said..." began Sepp.

She shook her head. "It is my firm belief he did not know of this to his last day. Salmor was a good man. He sincerely grieved my sister, but he did not know there had been a child.

"He married your mother some time later, and a year after that they celebrated your brother's birth as that of his first son. But he wasn't. It was Ardanna's child who was Salmor's first son. He lived for a few hours, the little mite; he drew his last breath a few minutes before his mother."

Cat knew a question was burning in the minds of the men sitting next to her, and she decided to speak it out loud. "Why didn't you say anything?"

"I was never sure of the Septimi, did not know whether they all had to be sons of the same mother for the seventh to be the Septimus, or no. Uncle did not know either. But more to the point was the uncertainty whether the child really had been Salmor's.

"If he was, then you, Sepp, are your *mother's* seventh son, but the *eighth* of your father—and the seventh son of the seventh son is Guy."

Ouska took a draught of her mintbrew.

"But I did not know whether it mattered, and I did not want to speak of it without absolute certainty. I had no wish to do an injustice to your father or cause unnecessary grief. So I bided my time, waited until you reached your full age. Watched, and waited."

Cat shot a look at Guy. He sat in his chair like a statue, his eyes fixed on his aunt.

"You came of age last year," Ouska said to him, "but I was still unsure. We hardly knew what to expect, any of us. All I saw was that you became more clumsy, more prone to hurting yourself and to breaking things. And is there not also something about your work? Something odd that began to happen right at that time?"

The image of the pottery pieces with the peculiar holes flashed through Cat's mind, and Guy frowned.

"Yes," he said slowly, "yes, there is. The day of my birthday, I had a kiln full of work which was riddled with holes, like something had bored its way through them in the firing. I don't know why it happens, but ever since, every time I fire there is at least one piece that has these holes running through it."

"He's been hiding them in the cupboard in the workshop," said Cat.

The wisewoman nodded. "I thought there was something, even though I had not seen it. But I could not be sure if any of it was a sign of your incipient power, even an odd one, or if it came from the hurt that wife of yours had left you with."

Guy winced.

"Haven't you wondered why that woman left you just then?" Ouska asked. "Haven't you asked yourself why she threw herself at you the way she did, enticed you to marry her? No, don't deny it—she went after you. I watched it happen, and did not stop it."

She turned her head and looked fully at Cat.

"You see, Guy," she continued, not turning her gaze from Cat, "I always knew you were to wed an Unissima." Now she finally looked away. "And that woman was the only there was. It galled me to see it—such an empty-headed, vain, foolish... No matter.

"She *was* Unissima, and it's my belief the Knowing told her you were more than a potter in the Wald. She kept her mouth shut about what she felt; she had that much sense, at least. Probably didn't want you snatched up by another woman. But she threw herself at you, she made you marry her. I won't say that you didn't come willingly—the young are foolish, powers or no. And she was beautiful, I'll give her that. Likely still is, from what the Knowing tells me."

There was a small light beginning to dawn in Guy's eyes.

"So then last June," Ouska continued, "you turned twenty-eight. She must have looked for some event, expected some great change—and when it didn't come, she threw a tantrum and left."

Guy made a noise, and his aunt looked at him with a shake of her head.

"Yes, of course I know that's what happened—you don't think I believe those foolish tale about your temper and her innocence? Don't forget I've known you since you were swaddled.

"You were left with the babe, and I had nothing to point to that told me whether you were the Septimissimus or not. So I waited yet longer. Until last week, when you, Sepp, reached your birthday, and less than nothing happened. Aside from that you vanished."

She picked up one of the brown bowl shards from the table.

"It's to do with these, isn't it?" she asked, with her direct glance at Guy and then Sepp.

"Yes," replied Cat for them. "It's what's left of a bowl, Guy made it."

"Of course," Ouska said. "I recall now, you told me of one that brought you here, did you not?"

"Yes. And there are more of them in the workshop."

The older woman got up off the bench.

"Show me," she said.

CHAPTER 24

T HE BOWLS WERE STILL where they had left them, on the floor of the workshop beside the open trap door, eerily glowing their turquoise blue as Cat shone the light of the lantern on them.

"Hmm," Ouska said, thoughtfully regarding the pots. She reached out a hand for them.

"NO!" both of the men yelled, leaping to stop her, Sepp with a grab for her wrist and Guy blocking the bowls with his arms.

"It's all right!" Cat called out without thinking, then found that she had spoken at exactly the same time, and in the same words, as Ouska. The two women's eyes met, and again Ouska gave Cat that small, approving nod.

"Don't fret yourselves," the older woman to her nephews. "The bowls will not harm me."

She removed Sepp's hand from her wrist, and her brown eyes looked steadily and firmly into Guy's turquoise ones. Finally, slowly and with obvious reluctance, he straightened up and took a step back.

Ouska bent and picked up a bowl. Sepp drew in a sharp breath; it was the twin to the bowl that had taken him away and brought Cat to this place.

The wisewoman cupped her hands around the bowl and let her gaze slide into its depths.

Cat could hear Guy's raspy breathing.

Glancing at him from the corner of her eyes, she saw that he trembled, staring at his aunt's hands. She turned her gaze fully on him. He looked up, and the fear in his eyes hit her with an almost physical force.

It's all right, she told him silently, *it's all right. Don't fret, don't be afraid. It's all right.*

His gaze held onto hers, taking courage; his breathing grew quieter, his shaking hands steadied.

Cat's eyes held his, soothing, calming. *At least he's not crushing any bones this time,* the little voice in the back of her mind said suddenly, and the corner of her mouth twitched up at the thought.

Ouska drew in a breath.

"Well," she said. She bent down and placed the bowl back on the floor with the others. "I believe I know what this is now."

"Why didn't you—" Sepp burst out.

"—get taken away?" Ouska finished. "Because I have no desire to leave."

The men stared, but Cat nodded softly. *Exactly.*

"There were pairs of them, were there not?" the older woman asked. "Two each that matched?"

"Yes," said Cat. "The matches to these two were taken to my world. And one bowl was broken, right at the beginning; the remaining one of that pair is still in there." She pointed into the storage hole.

Ouska nodded, as if that made perfect sense.

"Then this is how it is: the power (the magic, if you will, Catriona) is indeed in the glaze. There's something, I don't know what, that has combined in it, through the ash of the tree, the clay it soaked in, and the power of the Septimissimus.

"The bowls give a person who touches them the power to go from the place they are in to another. But only to a person who wants to go, who has a deep desire to leave. That is why the bowl I touched did not harm me, and they never harmed you yourself, Guy.

"But each bowl can only take a person one way. If you want to go back to where you came from, you need another bowl, by preference its match, but even a different one will do.

"There is a second use in each of the bowls, but not for the same person. So you, Catriona, came here with the bowl that Sepp went away with, did you not?"

"Yes," said Cat, who had been following Ouska's explanations and found they made perfect sense, "and he came back on Ashley's—Ashya's—bowl."

Ouska raised an eyebrow. "So that is where the woman is now? And how she left? No surprise."

She fixed her younger nephew with a stern gaze.

"So you and the woman left, because you wanted to be gone. Isn't that right?"

Sepp hung his head.

"Yes," he said to the floorboards. "I knew I had no powers, and so I was no use to the people as the Septimissimus. I thought it'd be better for everyone if I was gone..." He actually scuffed the toe of his shoe on the ground, and Cat had to bite back a smile at how much he looked like a kid caught with his hand in the candy jar.

But then he looked up.

"No," he said, "that's not really true. The truth is, I just *wanted* to be gone, wanted to be away from here. Just for me, myself, not for anyone else's sake. And then I was! So you're saying that is was my own wish that sent me away?" He ran a hand over his face. "Stars, I'm sorry. You must be furious with me."

Cat saw the look on Ouska's face. She didn't know if either of the men realized it, but it was perfectly clear that so far from being angry, Ouska, for one, was more than pleased with her nephew's insight and honesty.

"I think you've learned your lesson," the wisewoman said mildly.

"Have I ever!" said Sepp. "If there hadn't been another bowl to hand, I would have been stuck, like..." He looked at Cat, and his voice trailed off. She could practically see the gears turning in his head. "Wait!" he suddenly said. "If there's still that second bowl of the set here, couldn't Cat go back home on it?"

"She could," agreed his aunt. "She could also take the other matching bowl along, which would enable that woman to come back again." Her tone was bland, simply explaining facts, not suggesting a course of action.

Cat shot a look at Guy. He did not seem to have heard the last few sentences. His lips were pressed together hard, his eyes bleak. Turning away from the bowls on the ground, he limped over to the unlit fireplace and stared blindly into the empty grate.

"So it *was* my fault then," he ground out through his teeth.

An angry spark came into Ouska's eyes, and Cat suspected that it mirrored a look just like it in her own.

"Yes," said the older woman curtly. "Of course it was your fault that a selfish woman did not get her own way and had to take her foolishness to another place—where, I have no doubt, she is well served with it. Of course it was your fault that your brother lost his temper and wanted to get away from his home. Of course it was your fault that your powers, which you didn't even know you had, served other people for just the purpose they wanted." She snorted. "Did you not hear one word of what your brother just said? I wish you would stop this foolishness, boy, right this moment."

She marched past him through the workshop door into the cottage.

Cat and Sepp looked at each other.

"She's right, you know," Sepp said slowly, addressing his brother's back. "I did get what I wanted. I wanted to leave, and leave I did. And it's done me good, I think. The same goes for Ashya. Of course," he added slyly, "we can always bring her back with that other bowl, if you really want her back that much."

Guy whirled around.

"I don't—"

Sepp grinned, and Cat realized he'd been winding up his brother on purpose. It certainly had snapped him out of his gloom.

"Come on," Sepp said, clapping Guy on the shoulder as he walked past him. "I think Aunt is leaving."

Cat followed them into the cottage. Ouska was on the far side of the room, gathering her things to get ready to go. She picked up her cloak from the rocking chair, setting it gently rocking back and forth.

Sepp stared at the chair; then with wide eyes he looked at his brother.

"Guy! If I'm not—not *it*, I can make furniture! I no longer need to hide it, I can have a workshop, I can make whatever I want..." His voice trailed off.

"But Guy cannot," Cat finished. *'I'm a craftsman,'* she heard him saying in her memory, *'my work is who I am.'* "Ouska—it's not right! Does Guy really have to give up his pottery? Why?"

The older woman shook her head.

"I don't know it for certain," she said, "but I cannot believe it. I agree with you, Catriona, it does not seem right that it should be so."

"The Knowing?"

Ouska nodded. "That, but also, I believe this is one of those myths that have sprung up around the Septimus, that he *must not* follow a trade. I've always found it doubtful. It's true enough that Salmor never did, nor has any other Seventh Septimus we heard of. But Salmor never *wanted* to, he was happy in what he did. But he was a Septimus, not the Septimissimus. We have no way of knowing whether what's true for one is also true for the other."

Cat nodded vigorously. That fit exactly with what she thought herself.

"Guy is *good* at what he does," she said.

"Yes," Ouska agreed, "he is a gifted potter, no doubt about that. It seems wrong for him to lay down his craft. One gift is not paid for by another; that's why we call them gifts, not merchandise." She gave Guy a shrewd look. "And stop thinking anyone was harmed by you making things, boy. The only one who was hurt was you, and that's because you take it all harder than you should."

She swung her cloak around her shoulders.

"It'll take some time for you to get used to it, that's all, and find where you true gift lies, the one you can serve the people with—aside from the one that keeps us all in pots and jars, that is.

"What with those bowls, I'm beginning to suspect that your strength is in reinforcing, in bolstering what is already there. The bowls only work for someone who already wants to go, not for those who don't. Your hands give form, they shape what is there."

Ouska took Cat's right hand in hers and ran her brown thumb over the back of Cat's knuckles. Then she looked at her nephew.

"And what's more," she said, "I believe that at times where there is damage, your hands can heal. They not only shape, they make whole."

Guy had dropped back into his chair at the table, as if his weight was too much for his legs to bear, and he drew his hand down over his face, as if he were trying to rub away the strain and fatigue of the last few hours.

Cat gazed at him absentmindedly, Ouska's words running through her head. Suddenly she gave a little snort of laughter.

Guy looked up in surprise.

"Sorry," she said, "I just had a funny thought. You said you're dyslexic, Guy, right?"

"Dys-what?"

"You said you have trouble reading because the letters jump around on the page? We call that 'dyslexic' where I come from. It usually means you have trouble spelling, too."

He nodded with a slight frown, trying to follow her train of thought.

"Well, it seems your *gift* is dyslexic, too! You're meant to be a healer, a whole-maker, w-h-o-l-e." She flexed the fingers of her right hand that he had healed so recently. "But instead, you've become a hole-maker, h-o-l-e—that's why there have been holes in your pottery every since you turned twenty-eight!"

Sepp looked from Cat to his brother, his lopsided grin forcing its way out of the corner of his mouth. He tried to suppress a chortle, but it burst out with a loud guffaw.

Guy's expression changed from consternation to surprise to dawning comprehension, until he dropped his face into his hands and his shoulders shook with helpless laughter.

Ouska chuckled. She wrapped her cloak more tightly around herself and picked up her lantern. Turning down the flame a little, she shone its light on the little girl on the bed, then she turned to look at her nephews.

Sepp laughed up into her face, and she smiled at him in return.

Then she laid her hand on Guy's shoulder and looked down at him, a tender look full of pride and pleasure. Cat was not sure if the wisewoman said the words aloud, but she heard them as clearly as if Ouska had spoken them right beside her ear.

You can heal now, son.

Then the woman turned to Cat, her brown eyes looking straight into Cat's own. A look passed between them as between equals.

You will care for them, it said, *I can trust you.*

You can trust me, Cat's eyes answered back. *I will care for them.*

Ouska turned, and she lighted her way out of the cottage into the night.

CHAPTER 25

"P HEW!" SEPP TURNED TO the fire and hung the kettle back on the crane. "More mintbrew needed here. Unless there's any of Uncle's jack?" He shot a hopeful look at his brother.

"Mintbrew!" said Cat firmly. "Regardless of any availability of booze, I need more tea. And so do you," she said to Guy. "You look all done in."

He gave her his crooked smile, and she realized that the drawn look had gone from his face. His eyes had cleared, and there was peace in them. What a tremendous weight had been lifted from him! Cat smiled back at him, delighted.

Suddenly she thought of something.

"Won't this make things a bit awkward with your name, Sepp?"

"How do you mean?"

"Well, Sepp—it's short for Septimissimus, isn't it? You can hardly be called that if you're not him, even if it *is* your name."

"It's not his name," Guy said from his corner. "We just always called him that. His given name is Risyl."

"Oh!" That was certainly—unusual.

"*His* name," Sepp grinned and pointed at Guy, "is Dyniselm."

Cat blinked. "Is that normal here, calling people something completely different than their actual name?"

Guy shrugged.

"Sometimes. Certainly not unheard of. Don't they do that where you come from?"

"I suppose," Cat said. "I mean, sometimes we call people by their titles rather than names, of course—like you say Aunt, but her name is Ouska. What about Uncle?"

"Sardor!" chorused the brothers together.

"And—" Cat's eye fell on the sleeping baby on the bed, "and Bibby?"

"Ysbina!"

"Yes, that's a big name for such a little person." Cat smiled down at the little girl and reached out to gently brush back the red curls, which were plastered to the round forehead. The baby was sleeping hard.

"You know," Cat said thoughtfully, "if it wasn't for Ashley—Ashya—there would *be* no Bibby."

The men exchanged a glance.

"True," said Guy quietly.

Cat did not want to say what she had to say next.

"Maybe," she brought it out hesitantly, "maybe I *should* go back, and bring her the other bowl? Maybe she needs to come back here and be with her child. Maybe Bibby wants her, and maybe she..."

"Pffft!" said Sepp. "Not Ashya. You should have heard her when—oy, oy, oy, the kettle!"

He shot over to the hearth, where the kettle hissed and spat boiling water into the fire beneath it, sending up great swaths of steam. He danced from foot to foot to avoid the hot splashes, fishing for the fireplace crane with the poker and trying to stay out of its way at the same time.

Cat looked at Guy. There was a twinkle of amusement in his eyes, and her lips twitched in response. He gave a snort that turned into a chortle, and then they both burst out laughing, howling until Guy was breathless and the tears ran down Cat's face.

"Fine, make fun of me!" said Sepp indignantly, refilling the teapot with mintbrew.

"Oh, it's not you!" gasped Cat, trying to catch her breath. The tension of the last few hours—the last few days, and weeks—had dissolved right into that laughter.

"Oh yes, it is!" cried Guy, and it set them both off again, laughing until they were clutching their sides and wheezing.

Sepp shook his head indulgently.

"And you haven't even had any applejack yet." He put the teapot on the table. "Speaking of which, dear brother, when you have a breath..."

"Storage... hole!" Guy managed to gasp out through his chortles and snorts, weakly waving a hand in the direction of the front door.

Sepp apparently knew what Guy meant. He knelt down in the far corner of the cottage, and beneath the storage shelves he opened another trap door (*I might have known,* thought Cat). Triumphantly he extracted a good-sized brown pottery jug with a cork stopper.

"There we are," he said with satisfaction. He worked the stopper out of the bottle and poured a generous splash of the amber liquid into the bottom of each mug. Topping it up with mintbrew, he passed a mug to each of them.

"Here you are," he said, "Uncle Seppy's applemintjackbrew."

Cat wiped her streaming eyes on the sleeve of her blouse and raised her mug.

"To the Sepp, to the Septimissimus, the—oh, I don't know what else." She giggled weakly, then took a sip from the hot brew, letting the fiery liquor burn down her throat.

"To the Sepp!" and "To the Septimissimus!" responded the brothers, raising their cups to each other and taking rather deeper draughts of them than Cat had done.

"You know," she said, considering, "you could still go by Sepp. I had a Great-grandfather who was called that; I think with him, it was short for Joseph. Then we wouldn't have to get used to calling you something different."

"Brilliant!" cried Sepp delightedly. "I'll be the Joe-Sepp! To the finder of names and bowls and potters, to the Cat!" He raised his mug for another deep draught.

"Catriona," responded his brother, much more quietly. He raised his cup to Cat and drank, an intense light in his eyes as he looked at her. Cat felt a little tingle run down her spine.

Sepp cracked open his mouth in a tremendous yawn.

And suddenly, Cat realized that yet again, she was alone at night with two men, in a single-room cottage, which sported all of *one* wooden platform bed.

Ouska had left her with them, and Cat knew she had done it fully intentionally. *Probably her idea of humour*, she thought. *Or maybe she has something up her sleeve.*

Well, Cat could cope. But she was *not* going to share the bed with either of them. Especially Sepp, he was already half a sheet to the wind. Was there such a thing, half a sheet? Three sheets to the wind, she knew that, but what did you say when it was less than that?

Cat, shut up, she told herself. *You're about a quarter sheet in that direction yourself, or you wouldn't babble on in your head like this.*

"So." She cleared her throat and smiled brightly. "Where do I sleep tonight?"

The brothers looked at each other in surprise. Apparently the thought of sleeping arrangements hadn't crossed their minds either.

But then Sepp's face cleared. "Ohhh," he cried, stabbing a finger into the air, "not a problem! Prod a noblem! You and me, Guy, we roll up in little blankety heaps on the floor, we'll be cozy and snugs as rug in bugs..." He trailed off, blinking a little confusedly. "Blankety blugs..." he tried again, twirling his finger in a wobbly circle.

Guy reached out a hand and gently cuffed his brother upside the head.

"Shut up, you're drunk," he said dispassionately, taking the jug of liquor from Sepp's unresisting grasp. "But he's right," he said to Cat with an apologetic smile, "it's not really a problem. He and I will take the floor, if you don't mind sharing the bed with Bibby. She's used to sleeping there."

With you, thought Cat. Aloud she said, "As long as she won't mind? And—well, can your leg take it? Else I could sleep on the floor, too, you know." *At least I think I can.*

Guy had a surprised look on his face again, and he rubbed his injured knee.

"It's a lot better now—even better than just an hour ago!" he said. "In fact, it's completely better, I can't feel anything wrong!" He bent his leg back and forth at the knee. "I wonder what happened? You know, I think it was when..."

"...when your aunt left?"

"Yes! But how did you—"

Cat gave a tiny shrug. She couldn't explain what she had heard, or not heard, as it were; how she had simply *known.*

Guy got easily to his feet, leaned his hand on his knee and rotated it side to side, testing its restored mobility. "Yes, the floor it is," he said, "definitely."

He looked down at his brother, who had pillowed his head on his arms and was snoring softly. "Idiot," he said affectionately, and went to get some blankets from the chest against the wall.

CHAPTER 26

B IBBY WAS A WARM little bundle in Cat's arms through the night, curled up against her in the bed. So much more comfortable than the chair, even though that was magical. No, it wasn't, after all. Sepp was not the Septimissimus who made magical crafts. He was just very, very good at what he did. Guy, on the other hand—Cat was not going to think about Guy.

Sepp was snoring; probably an effect of the applejack. He didn't seem to have much of a head for alcohol. Cat heard Guy stirring, then a soft thump as he poked his brother to make him be quiet. Sepp grunted and snuffled, and the sounds told Cat he had rolled over. The snoring ceased, to be replaced by the deep, even breathing of the two sleepers, their rhythm offset from each other just a bit.

Cat smiled into the darkness, hugged the baby closer, and drifted back to sleep.

The sound of crashing crockery startled her upright. Sunlight streamed through the windows, and Cat stared around her, disoriented. On the floor, the men were struggling to their feet, obviously just as sleep-drunk as Cat herself. Memory came flooding back: the night, the conversation, the revelation of Guy as Septimissimus, of Bibby's mother, the explanation of the bowls.

The bowls! Bibby!

Cat swung her feet off the bed, hurriedly tugging down the chemise she wore for a nightshirt down to her knees. She grabbed the blanket from the bed, wrapped it around her like a shawl, and ran after Sepp and Guy into the workshop, where the noise had come from.

She pushed her way past the men, who stood stock-still in the doorway, and there was the little girl by the table, standing amidst the shards of Cat's return bowl. The glaze still glowed a faint turquoise on some of the pieces, but it was rapidly dulling to the rusty brown of the spent bowls.

Cat's eye flew to the turquoise gleam of the second bowl, clasped in Bibby's little hands.

"Bibby, no!" she cried, but before she could get to her, Bibby had raised the bowl as high above her head as she could stretch, and then hurled it to the floor with all her might. The turquoise dish shattered into a hundred pieces.

"*Boom*!" said the little girl, thoroughly satisfied.

"Oh Bibby!" wailed Cat, "What have you done?"

And suddenly she knew. She knew exactly what Bibby had done, and she also knew why. A warm feeling spread through her from her head to her toes.

"Well," she said, almost gleefully, "there goes my return ticket." She took that last step towards Bibby and scooped her up in her arms. "You little monkey, you!" She tickled the little girl's belly and made her giggle.

Bibby turned her large turquoise eyes on Cat.

"Bo bo fump!" she said importantly.

"Yes, the bowls went thump," confirmed Cat. "And now we'll have to clean them up." She looked at the smashed pieces on the floor, now all a dull rust colour, and then turned to Guy and Sepp, who stood in shock, staring at the shards.

"You can blink now," she said. Then she stepped in front of Guy and looked him straight in the eyes. "Bibby did that on purpose, you know," she said seriously. "She does not want her mother back; she is happy here with—with you. You see?"

Guy stared at her for another second, then he shook his head and blinked hard several times. He rubbed his hands over his face, drawing them down his cheeks and leaving his fingers pressed against his mouth for just a moment. It was as if with the gesture, he had wiped away the last remaining traces of the darkness and hurt that had had him in their grip for so long, and such a light began to shine from his eyes that Cat found it almost hard to look at.

"Bibby, Karana!" He stretched out his arms to his little girl.

"Bubba!" Bibby launched herself out of Cat's arms at her father.

He caught her, wrapped his arms around her, and held her tight. Bibby buried her face against his throat, her arms wrapped around his neck, squeezing as close as she could. They stood like this for a minute, perhaps two, Guy's head bent over his little daughter, his darker red curls falling over her light feathery ones.

Cat found she had a large lump in her throat.

Sepp cleared his throat with a *hrrrumph*. "Who's doing the cleaning up?" he said, his voice studiedly casual. There was a suspicious sheen of moisture in his eyes.

"You are," said Cat, sniffling a little through her smiles. "I have no idea where to find a broom."

There were choking noises coming from Guy. It looked like the hug had turned into a game of Squeeze-the-Daddy. Bibby refused to let go of her hold on his neck, clinging on in as tight a stranglehold as she could manage, giggling. Guy stuck out his tongue, rasping his mock choking breaths while trying to pull her away from his neck, but she stuck like a limpet.

Finally he resorted to counterattack. The long fingers of one hand spanned her small back, his thumb tickling her under one arm, the tip of the middle finger under the other, while at the same time he put his lips to her pudgy cheek and blew a loud raspberry. Bibby squealed loudly and let go.

Guy swung her out, holding her at arm's length over his head, where she squeaked and giggled, waving her little arms and legs. When he brought her back down and stood her on her feet, both father and daughter wore smiles of pure happiness.

The little girl toddled off to the cottage, and Guy went to follow her.

"Broom—corner, door," he said over his shoulder to his brother.

Sepp found a bristle broom next to the door to the privy, and a shovel-like scoop beside it.

"Here, hold that, will you?" he said, handing the scoop to Cat. Oh, of course, a dustpan. Clutching the blanket around her shoulders with one hand, Cat crouched on the floor and held the scoop for Sepp as he swept shards into it.

"Where to?" she asked.

"There's a crackpot bin by the kiln. Here, I'll take it."

"No—no, it's all right. I'll do it."

Carefully, in her bare feet, Cat picked her way over the ground, wet with morning dew. Yes, there is was, a small wooden bin half full of broken pieces and warped pots.

She looked down at the scoop in her hand, full of rusty brown pottery shards. There, that one came from "her" bowl, the one that was meant to have taken her back to her own world. It was small, only an inch or two across, but the curve of the rim made it clear which of the two pots it had belonged to. Cat carefully picked it out, wrapping her fingers around it protectively. Just a memento.

But those, they were the shards that belonged to Ashya's bowl. On an impulse, Cat pulled back the scoop, and with an overarm swing worthy of a professional baseball pitcher she smashed the contents into the bin. Not quite good enough. She reached into the bin, took out a large, heavy, brown crock with a big crack running through the bottom, and hurled it down onto those shards as hard as she could. The crash was magnificent.

"So there!" Cat said with a satisfied nod.

Suddenly she became aware of what she was doing. Embarrassed, she looked behind her, but the open doorway into the shop was empty. Sepp must have gone back into the cottage; that was a relief.

Except that she wouldn't really mind all that much if *Sepp* had seen her act silly. Guy, on the other hand...

Don't go there, Cat.

Cat collected her clothes and a comb from the cottage and went out back to get dressed. When she came back inside, breakfast preparations were underway. Sepp had stoked the fire, and he was setting a large black iron pot on three little legs into the embers.

"Oats in the storage hole?" he asked Guy over his shoulder as he opened the trap door in front of the shelf. Without waiting for an answer, he extracted a small sack made of tightly woven canvas. "When's the last time you used this? Probably before I left, wasn't it."

Guy snorted dismissively.

"You're not the only one who can cook, you know. Get off your high horse and get on with the porridge, my offspring is starving."

The starving offspring was showing her acute suffering by dancing around the cottage, whirling in circles until she got dizzy and plopped onto her plump little bottom.

"Fump!" she said, then got up to begin again, singing to herself, "Bibbyfump, Bibbyfump, Bibbyfump..."

"She's adorable," Cat said, watching her. "And so cheerful."

"Yes," said Guy, a tone of fond pride in his voice. "It's not much puts her out of humour. Mind you, when something does, she can throw a temper tantrum with the best of them. Don't know where she gets it." He caught the little girl in mid-whirl and bore her off to the corner to change her out of her nightshirt into her daytime tunic. (Cat had a brief vision flitting through her head of Ryan, his mouth curled into a sneer as he referred to the kids in her library storytime as "snotty rug rats". But it was a very brief flash—she could barely recall his face anymore. Goodbye, Ryan, and most excellent riddance to you.)

Last night's mugs and the teapot were still sitting on the table, as Cat went to get out the dishes for breakfast.

"I guess we can re-use the mugs. Are we going to need the—what do you call this, anyway?" She gestured at Guy with the teapot.

"The brewpot? Brewpot, of course. Why, what do you call it?"

"Teapot!" replied Sepp and Cat simultaneously. She looked at him; he seemed to have learned a thing or two in her world. What exactly had gone on between him and Nicky in those few days they had been together?

"Tea-pah!" repeated Bibby, delighted at a new word to add to her vocabulary.

"Yes, teapot!" said Cat. "Look, we even have a song about it." She stood in front of Bibby, put her right hand on her hip, stuck her left in the air beside her head, and in her best storytime manner began: "I'm a little teapot, short and stout…"

By the time the porridge was cooked, Bibby-the-teapot was tipping herself over and pouring herself out with the best of them, and she had to be forcibly sat on the bench to eat her breakfast or she would never have stopped.

For all her psychic powers (no, her Unissima's gift, Cat reminded herself), she was still just a little girl like any other. And Cat loved her.

CHAPTER 27

A FTER BREAKFAST, SEPP TOOK Bibby outside to play. It was rather obvious that he did it more to escape his brother's teasing about the burnt-on crust in the bottom of the porridge pot than to entertain his niece, but the little girl didn't care. "Uncayepp, Uncayepp," she sang, as she happily rode out the door on his back. He was still wearing his other-world's clothes; the jeans and t-shirt somehow suited him.

Cat helped Guy with clearing up the dishes and straightening the cottage, but the longer they worked, the more strained the silence between them became.

What now, Cat, what now? Guy was fully recovered, he didn't need her help anymore. Sepp was returned, and the mystery of his disappearance cleared up. Cat no longer had a role to play in this world. She was stuck on an alien planet with the space program discontinued. She couldn't even go home and pick up where she left off; the travelling bowls were broken...

Guy cleared his throat.

"Cat—Catriona?"

Cat looked at him. There was a serious, uncertain expression in his eyes; he swallowed convulsively.

"There—there is something I—I want to... Just come, please." He turned on his heel and strode through the door into the workshop.

Cat wrinkled her brows. Now what was he up to?

She followed him into the workshop, and found him bent over the trap door that had hidden the bowls.

Oh! There *was* a bowl left! What...

Guy straightened up, the pot cupped in his strong, slender hands, glowing its eerie turquoise blue. He stepped over to the table and placed it carefully on the canvas surface. His head bent, he stared down at it for a long moment.

Then he raised his head and looked straight at Cat.

"This is yours. I will not keep you here, I will not hold you. If you want to leave, this is your path. If you want to go," his voice wavered slightly, "then go."

His gaze turned back to the bowl, and he half raised his hand to reach for it—as if he wanted to snatch it back, retract his offer... But he clenched his fist and pulled it back against his chest, then abruptly straightened up.

"Farewell, Catriona," he said, his voice barely audible, and without looking at her, his back ramrod straight, he walked out of the shop.

Cat blinked. He had given her no time to respond, no time to think. No time to feel, to sense what she needed to do.

Averting her eyes from the bowl on the table, she turned and slowly walked back into the cottage. The rocking chair called to her from the corner. She leaned back into it, and it cradled her back, gently, kindly, as she softly swayed back and forth.

Guy, Bibby, Sepp.

Ryan, Nicky, Ashya.

Ouska, Uncle.

Guy, Bibby.

Guy.

ele

It was nearly an hour later that Sepp and Bibby came back inside.

"She needs a nap," Sepp said, setting the little girl on her feet, "she's getting cranky."

"No ganky!" protested Bibby with a pout, her voice tearful.

"No, of course not." Sepp sat her on the end of the bed and took off her shoes. "Where's Guy?"

"I don't know," said Cat, slowly and softly. "He—walked out."

"Oh?" Sepp gave Cat a sidelong glance, one eyebrow quirked up. He picked up the baby, put her in the bed, and tucked the blanket around her.

Bibby grizzled. "No nap!"

"No, no nap," Sepp agreed. He leaned down, kissed the little girl on the forehead, then gently stroked his hand downwards over her face. Her eyelids closed, and in a few breaths she was asleep.

Her uncle smiled his crooked smile down at her. Then he sat down on the bench, leaned backwards onto the table with his elbows, and directed his turquoise gaze at Cat in a long, straight look.

"Well?"

She met his look with one of her own, then drew a deep breath. There was one more thing she needed to know.

"Sepp? Who, or what, is Karana?"

He looked surprised.

"Karana? How... Oh, I suppose you heard us call the babe that. It's nobody in particular, just a pet name we have for people that we, well..." He sounded a little embarrassed. "It's—private. We don't use it in public. If you heard us saying it, well, you're probably the first person ever, outside of the family."

"Where does it come from?"

"Father invented it, for Mother. He gave it its meaning."

"Which is...?"

Now Sepp looked distinctly sheepish.

"If you must know," he said, avoiding Cat's eyes, "it means 'My Dearest Love and Delight of my Heart.'" He glanced at Cat out of the corner of his eye, and when he saw that she didn't burst into derisive laughter, he shrugged, the smile flashing out again. "I know it's sentimental, but that's Father. Or that *was* Father, rather. So much like Guy, everything is drama. But there you are, that's what it means."

"You started to say 'people that we...' You mean people that you—you care about?"

"Yes."

There it was.

Cat looked down at her fingers, pleating and unpleating the fabric of her skirt.

"Did—did Guy ever call *her* that?"

"Who? His wife?" Sepp looked thoughtful. Then he shook his head. "I doubt it. Mind you, of course I wasn't there when they were alone, but—I just doubt it, that's all."

Cat felt a blush rising in her cheeks, but she had to know.

"Sepp—did he love her?"

The young man's eyes were serious.

"I think he tried," he said quietly. "He tried his hardest. He was flattered when she went after him, of course; what man wouldn't be? She's a looker. He was infatuated for a while, a short while. But after that, I think, it became like trying to love a statue. Because that's what she was—still is. Perfect to look at, cold, and hard." He leaned forward, putting his elbows on his knees. "She doesn't have half the beauty you have. You're alive, and warm, and... Well, I've seen the way he looks at you. You're the best thing that's happened to him, ever."

Cat's head, her cheeks on fire with a fierce blush, came up at that.

"But—he wants me to go!"

Sepp frowned.

"What makes you think that?"

"Come, look," Cat said, getting up from the rocker and leading the way into the workshop. She gestured at the bowl. "See? He put it out, for me to use."

Sepp started back at the sight of the pot, but then he pulled himself together and stepped closer.

"It still scares me," he admitted. "But, Cat—what exactly did Guy say?"

"He put it there, and said that it was for me, and if I wanted to leave, I should leave." She stopped. Suddenly she knew. Why had she not known before? She knew! Her heart filled with a light, warm, bubbly feeling that expanded and spread through her whole body.

"Sepp!" she cried, delighted with him, delighted with herself. "Sepp, *it won't work!* The bowl won't work, because it only works for someone who wants to leave—*and I don't!* I am staying! I'm not going anywhere, I'm staying here!"

She was so happy she could have hugged him. She did not know what she was going to do with herself in this strange world, this world of magic and Septimi and small girls who had second sight, but she knew she belonged there. She would stay, she would find a place to live, she would move in with Ouska and learn her craft, she would...

Cat suddenly became aware of an odd look on Sepp's face. An intent look, half puzzled, half determined.

"Cat," he said slowly, as if thinking aloud, "Cat, do you think it might work for me?"

And again, Cat knew.

"It's Nicky, isn't it." It was a statement, not a question. She considered. "I won't ask what happened, I'm sure you'll tell me sometime. Yes," she said, positive now, "the bowl will work. Take it, and when you get there, be careful. But you'll know what to do.

"Oh, and one thing,"—she had no idea where this sudden thought came from, but she knew it was important to tell him—"Nicky is terrified of mice."

And this time she did hug him, one tight, strong hug, from sister to brother.

Then Cat stepped back, picked up the glowing turquoise bowl from the table, and held it out to Sepp.

"Goodbye, Risyl!"

"Goodbye, Cat." He reached for the bowl, and as his hands touched it, she just saw his eye close in a wink.

And then he was gone.

CHAPTER 28

C AT DREW A DEEP breath.

Now what, Cat?

Wait, that was what. Wait, and watch over the sleeping little girl in the next room. Something inside of Cat was tuned to Bibby, knew that the baby was still sound asleep on the bed.

Cat let her eyes travel around the workshop.

The shelves with the fired, unglazed pots.

The cupboard that held the beautiful blue and green and pierced pieces, where she had found the mysterious broken necklace.

The work table; the drying shelves with the half-finished wares.

Her gaze slid to the trapdoor in the floor, the trap door that had concealed the turquoise bowls. Would there ever be more of them? *Maybe not ones exactly like it,* the voice inside of her said, *but others, with different powers.*

The wheel. Cat thought of how Guy's strong fingers had shaped the cups, had pulled form from formlessness.

She sat down on the wheel bench, her hands resting on the surface of the wheelhead. It turned, very gently. She stretched out a toe and nudged the flywheel. It idly spun into slow, lazy motion. She let her fingers trail along the edge of the wheelhead as it silently turned around, and around...

Steps sounded along the outside of the building. Guy's steps. Cat's heart leapt into her throat.

The latch rattled, and the door creaked open.

Guy stepped into the workshop, hope and apprehension mingled on his face. His gaze went straight to the table.

The bowl was gone, the table empty.

His shoulders slumped, and as he turned to leave the room, his face was full of bereft hurt, of disappointed longing.

Longing for her. Silly man. Why did he not look up?

"Guy," she said softly.

He whirled around, and he saw her. His eyes lit up in a blaze of turquoise, incredulous joy suffusing every line of his face. In three strides he crossed the room, stopping himself hard in front of her where she slid off the wheel bench.

"Catriona! Cat—you're here..."

"Yes," she said, smiling up at him, "I'm here."

"But—but the bowl..."

"I gave it to Sepp. He needs it, he has unfinished business back in my world. My *old* world. And don't fret," she added, "he'll come back. I know."

"You know..." he said softly. "You are—you are Unissima."

"Yes, I'm Unissima. I belong here, my place is here. The bowls have no effect on me any longer."

He took a deep breath, then another to steady himself.

"I—I went to the village. I was hoping—wishing—" His voice trailed off, then he began again. "When I saw the bowl was gone, I thought I had made a fool of myself... You see, I got—this."

He reached into the pocket of his vest and brought out a small pouch made of soft washleather. He loosened the drawstring and reached into the pouch.

His slender fingers drew out a silver chain. Cat watched, mesmerized, as the bright links slipped out of the bag, one by one, and finally revealed on their end a silver pendant. A small, beautiful, filigreed cat.

Guy's turquoise eyes looked down into Cat's.

"Catriona, Karana," he said softly, "marry me."

And Cat knew what to answer.

"Yes, Dyniselm Septimissimus, I marry you."

With trembling fingers Guy opened the clasp of the necklace, and held it out to Cat. She gathered her hair and held it up; he clasped the chain around her neck and settled the silver cat against the hollow of her throat.

And before she could think, she was crushed in his arms, his lips coming down on hers in a kiss that took what little was left of her breath away. Cat didn't mind one bit.

Suddenly a small body hurled itself against their knees.

"Bibby up!" demanded a little voice.

Guy raised his head and laughed. Keeping his left arm firmly wrapped around Cat, he reached down with his right and grasped the little girl under her arm. Cat reached down with her right, and together they pulled the baby up and held her between them.

Bibby beamed at them.

"Bubba," she said, "Gah," patting her father on the cheek with one hand and Cat with the other.

Then she pulled back a little, looked from one of them to the other, and came to a conclusion.

"Bubba Mumma!" she said, and she wrapped her little arms around their necks as far as she could reach.

NOTE

All the remedies and technologies in this story, apart from the obviously magical ones, work in Cat's old world as well. Potters really did make glazes with a mix of ashes and clay; basil powder and garlic are antiseptic; and cider vinegar makes a good hair rinse if you've washed your hair with soap.

For Ouska's silver polish, use an aluminum dish such as a disposable pie plate or put some aluminum foil in the bottom of another dish, and then simply follow her method. It works.

But if you should you ever find a tree with turquoise blue bark, do please let me know if there are special properties in the ashes.

ACKNOWLEDGEMENTS

Seventh Son would never have seen the light of day, in its first or second edition, without the help of a number of wonderful people.

For the first edition, there were my husband Peter and daughter Anna, who read it first, helped me iron out the lumpy bits, never got tired of discussing the characters and plot twists, and through it all were unfailingly encouraging; my beta readers Christopher, Louise, and Desi; Lee Strauss, who showed me how this whole book publishing thing is done; and my editor Jennifer Ballinger, who taught me so much about good writing.

For the second round, the biggest shout-out goes to my friend, critique partner, and now editor E.L. Bates of Star-Dance Editing, who carefully picked over the manuscript and made sure it was as shinyperfect as we could make it between us.

And then there were all of you, my wonderful readers, who read the story and loved it and made it worthwhile to polish the story one more time.

THANK YOU.

ABOUT THE AUTHOR

Angelika M. Offenwanger lives in rural Western Canada with her family, two cats, numerous dust bunnies, and a small stuffed bear named Steve. She likes walking barefoot through the mud because she enjoys the squishy feeling between her toes.